## "Don't try to deny what's between us."

Alex took a purposeful step toward her as Sara raised her hands in a futile attempt to ward him off. But he merely smiled and caught her wrists.

Briefly she tried to struggle, but he said harshly, "It's too late, the fight's over." And he pulled her into his arms.

His mouth covered hers hungrily, claiming possession, allowing no resistance. Desperately Sara tried to break free, but she couldn't escape the passionate torment of his lips, searching, demanding a response.

She made a little sound deep in her throat and the hand she'd raised to hit him instead sank slowly onto his shoulder and crept around his neck....

OTHER
*Harlequin Romances*
by SALLY WENTWORTH

Many of these titles are available at your local bookseller
or through the Harlequin Reader Service.

For a free catalogue listing all available Harlequin Romances,
send your name and address to:

HARLEQUIN READER SERVICE,
M.P.O. Box 707, Niagara Falls, N.Y. 14302
Canadian address: Stratford, Ontario, Canada N5A 6W2

or use coupon at back of book.

# Liberated Lady

by

## SALLY WENTWORTH

## Harlequin Books

TORONTO • LONDON • NEW YORK • AMSTERDAM
SYDNEY • HAMBURG • PARIS

Original hardcover edition published in 1979
by Mills & Boon Limited

ISBN 0-373-02262-X

Harlequin edition published May 1979

# CHAPTER ONE

'No, no, she's holding the chocolate bar too tightly. We can't see the name on the wrapper. Tell her to hold it by her fingertips.' Sara gave a sigh of exasperation as the crew set up the shot for the eighth time.

Beside her in the director's box overlooking the television studio that she had hired for the morning, the vision mixer reset the screens while the floor manager below them acknowledged her instructions with a wave of his hand. 'Sorry, Miss Royle. We'll take it again.' His voice sounded flat and metallic over the headset she was wearing.

The cameramen joked among themselves as they repositioned their cameras, long trailing tubes of cable like umbilical cords snaking out behind them, while the sound technicians moved the booms into place, skilfully avoiding the scenery. A make-up girl carried her tray across to the pouting little girl who was the star of the advertising film and gave a last-minute touch to her hairstyle. At last they were ready and this time, fortunately, all went well; the child spoke on cue, looked as if she was really enjoying the new confectionery bar which hadn't yet started to melt under the hot lights, and even managed not to cover up the all-important brand name with her fat little fingers.

'Okay, I think that's in the bag. All we have to do now is add the opening jingle,' the vision mixer remarked with a relieved grin.

'Thank goodness. I was afraid we were going to overrun our time and have to pay everybody overtime rates. The boss would have been livid if we had—this contract has a tight budget. Lord, how I hate working with children,' Sara added. 'You can almost guarantee that something will go wrong. Either they're snivelling with a cold, crying with temper, or their mothers make such a fuss about their appearance that everything gets held up for ages.'

'Don't forget animals,' her companion reminded her. 'What about the time that dog grabbed the product and disappeared into the audience seats? It took us nearly an hour to catch him again.'

'Oh, don't remind me,' Sara said with a groan. 'That was one of my first assignments too. I don't know why the advertising agency didn't fire me there and then.'

'Probably because everyone else steered clear of the job and they pushed it on to a greenhorn,' he laughed.

Sara smiled back and then stood up to gather up her papers and put them into her documents case. The technician ran his eyes over her appraisingly, liking the look of her slim, long-legged figure in the fashionable full skirt and tweedy jacket, the swirl of shoulder-length fair hair that framed her delicately boned features and deceptively gentle brown eyes. Deceptive because he knew those eyes could quickly flame if any man tried to put her down or override her directions without a good reason for doing so, or just because she was a woman in a man's world.

'I'll leave you to wrap it up, Bill. I've got an appointment at two with a new client and I want to do some homework before I meet him.'

'Okay, Sara. I'll bring the finished film in later and drop it in your office.'

She thanked him and hurried out of the studios to

the car-park. If she made good time to the office she might be able to catch up on some paper work while she ate a sandwich lunch. She had been fully aware of the technician's appraisal, had in fact grown quite used to such scrutinies over the last few years as men had tried to weigh her up, wondering just how she had managed to reach a junior executive position in the very cut-throat world of advertising at the relatively early age of twenty-six. Many of them, as they hadn't failed to imply, thought that she had got there via the Managing Director's bed, but only she knew that she had had to fight twice as hard as a man would have done to attain and hold her position. She had started off by working as a secretary, but had got tired of being treated like a mindless idiot who could only obey orders, so had set out to prove herself and had eventually clawed her way to her present highly-paid and responsible position. There had been some hard knocks to take along the way, a lot of them, surprisingly, from other women who hadn't been so successful, but the knocks had made her harder, more self-reliant and more determined than ever to get where she wanted to be.

There was a frustrating hold-up in Baker Street, but at last she was through and had parked the car in her own reserved parking place in the underground car-park beneath the block in which her company had its offices. As she took the lift up to the fifth floor she was already going through the jobs that awaited her, sorting them into order of importance. There should just be time to go over the folio of poster designs for the cosmetics contract before she boned up on the new client. She strode along the corridor to the door with her name on it and stepped briskly through.

Her secretary looked up as she entered and was about to say something, but Sara interrupted her. 'Bring me the cosmetics company's folio as soon as you can, will you, Jane? And send out for my usual sandwiches. No time for lunch again, today, I'm afraid.' She turned to walk into her own inner office, and it was only then that she caught sight of the young girl in school uniform who had risen to her feet as Sara came in. 'Nicky! What on earth are you doing here? Why aren't you at school?' She stared at the girl in amazement.

'I—I wanted to talk to you.' The girl glanced un-certainly at the secretary and then looked at Sara appealingly.

'All right, come into my office. Jane, you'd better make that sandwiches and coffee for two.' Sara followed Nicky into the office and took off her jacket before seat-ing herself at her desk. She looked at her half-sister rather grimly, wondering what new problems she would have to cope with.

'Okay, let's have it. Why are you in London when you should be at boarding school in Kent?'

Nicky raised her head rather defiantly. 'I've left,' she said baldly. 'I've had enough of being treated like a child and having to wear this stupid uniform. You don't know what it's like being cooped up there,' she went on hastily as she saw the angry light that had come into Sara's eyes. 'The same old round of lessons week after week, the cliques among the other girls and the cattiness. Sara, I can't stand it there any longer! I just had to leave!'

'Did you really?' Sara's voice was sharp with anger. 'Well, you'll just have to go back again. Don't you realise you take your A levels next term? If you fail those you won't be able to get a place in a university.'

Biting her lip, Nicky looked pleadingly at her sister. They were not much alike, although they had had the same mother, Sara's mother having remarried after her father's death. Whereas Sara was fair, Nicky had light brown hair worn short and curly and her face and figure still showed a trace of teenage puppy-fat, but she could one day be quite pretty when she was properly groomed and made up. Rather haltingly she said, 'I know how much it means to you, Sara, but I'm sorry, I don't want to go to university.'

Sara's face became grimmer. 'Is this some whim or have you got a reason for saying that? You haven't been expelled, have you?' she asked sharply.

'No, nothing like that,' Nicky assured her hastily, and then flushed and looked away as Sara's eyes studied her.

'Come on, Nicky. Something's happened, and you'll have to tell me sooner or later. Or shall I phone the school and ask them?' she threatened.

'You don't have to do that.' The younger girl lifted her head and there was a curious little look of pride in her face as she said huskily, 'I've got a boy-friend.'

'Is that all?' Sara gave a laugh of relief. 'I'd been imagining all kinds of dire things! But you're not allowed to have boy-friends, are you? Did you get into a row when the teachers found out? Well, never mind, I'll try and square it with them; tell them you won't see him again and will be on your best behaviour from now on.'

'But you don't understand,' Nicky interrupted. 'I don't want to give him up. As a matter of fact,' she added defiantly, 'we want to get married!'

There was a brief, shattering silence into which only the noise of the traffic in the street below intruded.

'What did you say?' Sara asked disbelievingly.

'You heard what I said. Richard and I have fallen in love and we want to get married.' Nicky's voice rose as her defiance grew stronger.

'Love? You're not even old enough to know the meaning of the word!'

Her sister's face flushed. 'Yes, I do. I know that I love Richard and I want to spend the rest of my life with him.'

Sara tried to keep her voice calm. 'But you're only seventeen. And however strong you think your feelings are at the moment, I can assure you they won't last. In a few weeks' time you'll have fallen for some pop star or someone instead, and you'll look back on this Richard and wonder what on earth you saw in him. Who is he anyway? A pupil at a neighbouring school?'

'No, he's a student at London University. He's going to be a lawyer, and he's twenty.'

With a frown between her brows, Sara studied her sister. She had been Nicky's guardian for nearly four years now, ever since the terrible car crash that had left them both orphans. It had not been an easy responsibility; Sara knew what Nicky's father had wanted for her and she had tried to scrupulously follow his wishes, but it had caused her worries and problems at a time when her career had demanded her full attention. She had thought that this was just a schoolgirl/schoolboy romance, but if the boy was twenty ...? She said slowly, 'Have you told this boy about the money your father left you?'

Nicky tossed her head, flicking her fringe out of her eyes. 'Of course. We decided right from the beginning that we wouldn't have any secrets from each other.'

'I see.' Sara's voice hardened. 'And has it occurred to you that he might want to marry you just for the money? It's a great deal of money, you know, Nicky.'

'That's a horrid thing to say! I *know* he loves me.'

'No, that's just the point. You don't know. You're not old enough or experienced enough to tell the true from the sham.' Sara leaned forward earnestly. 'Look, you have to be sensible about this. If this boy really loves you then he'll want you to finish your education, not drag you away from it. You've got plenty of time; time to get your A levels and go to university and *then* get married. You've got the most marvellous opportunity to make something of your life, Nicky. You ought to grab it with both hands, not throw it away because some boy has kissed you and made you think you're a woman instead of a schoolgirl!'

Nicky looked down at her hands for a moment and then across at Sara. 'I know you only want the best for me, and I'm grateful, Sara, honestly I am. I know you want me to have all the opportunities you didn't have, but I don't *want* a career. It isn't my scene at all. I just want to marry Richard and live with him. A university education would be wasted on me. I haven't got your drive and ambition. I suppose I'm just the old-fashioned type who wants to get married and have kids.'

Sara looked at her sharply. 'You haven't—you haven't had sex with this boy, have you?'

Nicky's face went brilliant red and she hastily turned away as a tap came at the door and the secretary came in with a tray of sandwiches and coffee.

When the girl had gone, Sara said, 'Well?'

Her face still flushed, Nicky shook her head.

Sara looked at her intently for a moment, then said, 'Here, have something to eat.' She glanced at her watch and was acutely aware of the passing time. 'Look, Nicky, there's some work I just have to do. I'll give you the key of the flat and you can go and wait for me there, but heaven knows what time I'll be able to get away. I'll phone your headmistress and tell her where you are. I suppose you'd better stay in London tonight and I'll take you back to school tomorrow.' Seeing the obstinate look that came into her sister's eyes, she said exasperatedly, 'I'm sorry, Nicky, but there's no alternative. You're under age, and there's no way I'm going to give my consent to this utterly stupid idea. You go back to school tomorrow and I shall make sure that the teachers know that you're not to see this boy again.' Her voice softened and she reached out to touch the younger girl's hand. 'I know it seems harsh and Victorian, but believe me, it's for your own good.' When Nicky didn't answer she gave a little sigh and said, 'Eat your lunch.'

'I'm not hungry.'

'Look, if you're going to sulk you can do it somewhere else.' She fumbled in her bag. 'Here's the key and some money for a taxi. I'll be home tonight as soon as I can.'

Her face tight and unhappy, Nicky took the key and went quickly out of the office without a word. Sara stared after her for a moment, then shrugged her shoulders and picked up the dossier on the new client. One thing she had learned early in her career was how to shut out outside influences and concentrate singlemindedly on the job in hand, and soon she was immersed in her work, the problem of Nicky pushed to the back of her mind.

The new client proved to be very garrulous; he hadn't been pleased to find he had a woman to deal with, so Sara had to put herself out to convince him that she could do the job. Using her sex had come into it a little too—a thing she despised—but she had

found from bitter experience that it cut a lot of corners
and saved a great deal of time. As it was, because she
wanted to get away early and was so pushed for time,
she almost flattered and charmed the contract out of
him. But then he wanted to see the graphic artists' and
photographers' studios and it was late anyway before
she could get rid of him—and there was still the cosmetics folio to go through before she could go home.

She was still staring at her desk when Jane buzzed to
tell her that someone wanted to see her. 'It's a Mr
Alexander Brandon. He says it's most important he
sees you.'

'Tell him I'm not available. Find out what he wants
and if it's important he'll have to make an appointment, but not this week, I've got far too much on. And
then go home yourself, Jane. There's no point in our
both being stuck here.'

Sara went back to her task, but the buzzer went again
almost immediately. 'He won't tell me what he wants.
He says it's a personal matter.'

Annoyance in her voice, Sara said, 'I don't care what
you do, Jane, just get rid of him.'

Clicking off the intercom, she muttered under her
breath, angry that someone should expect her to see
him at this time of night, but she had hardly glanced
back at her work before the door burst open and a man
strode into the room, Jane close behind him.

'I'm sorry, Sara, I tried to stop him, but he just
brushed past me.'

'That's all right, Jane, just ring for the caretaker and
tell him to send someone up here to have an intruder
thrown out, will you please?' Sara spoke calmly, but
there were two bright spots of anger in her cheeks at
this rude eruption into her office.

The stranger strode purposefully across the room and put his hands on her desk, looming over and glaring at her. 'I'm afraid I'm not quite that easy to get rid of—isn't that the charming phrase you used, Miss Royle? And before you send for your minions to try to throw me out, a job they won't succeed in doing by the way, I think I'd better tell you that Richard French is my nephew.'

Sara stared at him as he leaned so menacingly close to her. 'Richard who?' she asked in complete bewilderment.

He sighed as if he were dealing with somebody very stupid. 'Richard French, the boy your sister wants to marry.'

'Oh!' Sara recovered a little and nodded to her secretary. 'All right, Jane, you can cancel that call. I'll deal with this. Go on home now.'

'I'll stay if you want me to,' Jane offered, looking rather apprehensively at the intruder.

'No, it's all right. I'll see you tomorrow. Goodnight.'

The girl withdrew and Sara turned to give her full attention to the man before her. He had straightened up and she saw that he was tall, about six feet two, she judged, with broad shoulders that balanced his height. He was wearing a well-cut grey suit and his dark, rather thick hair was brushed neatly back to reveal lean, almost autocratic features. Features that were set in an angry frown as he looked at her sardonically from his grey eyes.

'Won't you sit down, Mr ...? I'm afraid I didn't catch your name.'

'No, you were in too much of a hurry to bother to listen.' He hooked a chair forward and sat down, crossing his legs casually. 'My name's Brandon, Alex Bran-

don, and, as I said, Richard French is my nephew and
under my care. His parents farm out in Africa and I'm
responsible for him until he gets his degree. Then he's
on his own.'

'Well, if you're responsible for him, then I'd be
pleased if you'd keep him away from my sister,' Sara
said sharply. Alex Brandon opened his mouth to speak,
but she went on relentlessly, 'He may have sent you
here to plead his cause for him, but it won't do any
good. In fact I would have thought more of the boy if
he'd come here himself instead of sending you as his
emissary. And I may as well tell you right now that you
haven't a hope in hell of getting me to agree to this
ridiculous marriage. Your nephew may have wormed his
way into Nicky's affections, but if you think I'm going
to allow her to marry some fortune-hunting oppor-
tunist, then you're wrong, Mr Brandon, totally wrong!'

Alex Brandon still sat casually in his chair, but his
jaw had hardened and there was an unpleasant glint in
the grey eyes as he listened to her. 'Have you finished,
because I . . .?'

'No, I haven't,' Sara swept on. 'As your nephew was
too much of a coward to come here himself, then you
can give him this message; tell him to stay away from
Nicky. She may have given him the impression that she
would inherit her father's money when she marries,
but she can't do so unless she marries with my approval
and permission. And there's no way I'm going to let her
marry your parasite of a nephew just so that he can live
comfortably on Nicky's money while he's studying for
his degree—if he really is studying,' she added caustically.

'Oh, he's studying all right,' Alex Brandon leaned
forward, an angry note in his voice. 'Studying hard and

doing well until your sister came along and started throwing herself at him! Since then she's pestered him so much that he can't concentrate on his work and he's been getting into trouble with his college because she's always phoning him at inconvenient times and getting him to skip lectures so that he can meet her.' He rose to his feet and glared down at her disdainfully. 'That boy is in my charge and I don't intend to let him lose the chance of a promising career just because some silly little schoolgirl has got the nesting instinct. So you see, Miss Royle,' he added sardonically, 'we both want to see this unfortunate little affair come to an end, albeit for different reasons, as you would have found out if you'd had the good manners to ask me what I wanted instead of jumping to conclusions.'

Sara looked up at him as she assimilated what he had said, but before she could say anything, he added in an extremely sarcastic tone, 'And now that I've met you, Miss Royle, I can understand why your sister was only too eager to leave your guardianship, but she'll have to find someone other than Richard as her means of escape.'

'And just what is that remark supposed to mean?' There were bright spots of angry colour on Sara's cheeks as she gazed at Alex Brandon, her temper held tightly in check.

'It means, Miss Royle, that you are one of the most dictatorial and unfeminine women I've ever had the misfortune to meet. I'm willing to bet that you order your sister around and bully her into obeying you, telling her it's for her own good. The poor kid is probably frightened to death of you and willing to do anything to get away.'

'How dare you?' Sara, too, rose to her feet angrily.

'The relationship between my sister and me is nothing whatsoever to do with you!'

'It is when she tries to use my nephew as a means of getting away from it,' he said bluntly.

'Nicky is not trying to get away. We're on very good terms and she knows she can always come to me when she needs help.'

'Does she? And what help did she get from you this time? You hardly listened to her before ticking her off and sending her away. Too wrapped up in your damn job to even spare half an hour of your time!'

The hold on Sara's temper began to slip. 'You've got a cheek coming here and talking to me like that! If you had any sort of control over your nephew you'd make sure he kept to his studies instead of chasing after young girls. And I can guess who he learnt that from,' she added nastily.

'Can you indeed?' Alex Brandon leant forward, his hands on the desk. 'Well, you'll be happy to know that I wouldn't even look at your type. You career women are all the same—you're so busy beating men down in your fight to get to the top that you lose all your femininity. And you're so insecure and afraid of losing what you've gained that you browbeat others into doing what you want. Just like you browbeat your sister!'

Sara took a hasty step around the desk and faced him angrily. 'I don't have to justify my actions to you. And just what makes you think I didn't listen to her?'

'Because Richard was waiting for her outside. He wanted to see you together, but Nicky wouldn't let him —she evidently knows you very well. She was going to tell you about him and then call him in to introduce him to you. But you didn't even let her get that far! You told her not to be a naughty little girl and sent her off with a flea in her ear. She was so upset that Richard brought her to me.'

'And I suppose you welcomed them with open arms?' Sara asked sarcastically.

'No, but I didn't throw them out in the street!' he told her harshly. 'I cancelled all my engagements for the afternoon and listened to them, then I took them to a restaurant and left them there while I came on here. Neither of them had eaten all day, but I don't suppose you bothered to find that out either,' he added derisively.

Sara thought of the uneaten sandwiches and her hands balled into tight fists. For a moment she wished heartily that she were a man so she could knock the sneering look off Alex Brandon's face. 'Then just what did you come here for—other than to insult me, of course?'

'To try if we couldn't work out some way between us of persuading them to wait for a few years. They're both far too young and it just won't do until they've finished their education. I was going to suggest that you might take your sister abroad for a couple of months to give her something else to think about, but I can see that you're the last person to put yourself out for someone else,' he finished, his tone heavy with sarcasm.

'So why don't you take your precious nephew away instead?' she asked with deceptive mildness.

'That's out of the question at the moment, I'm afraid. I have some important business coming up in the next few weeks that I can't leave to anyone else.'

Sara looked at him sardonically. 'I see, it's all right for me to take a couple of months off and probably lose my job in the process, but your company, of course, is quite incapable of functioning without you.'

He flushed slightly. 'As a matter of fact it is. I'm . . .'

But Sara interrupted him angrily. 'Nobody's indispensable, Mr Brandon. You, and all the other male chauvinists like you, just think you are. And I have no time for self-opinionated, pompous bores, so unless you've got something constructive to say, I suggest you leave. I have a great deal of work to do before I go home and talk to Nicky. And you don't have to worry, because I shall make darn sure she doesn't ever marry your nephew. I wouldn't wish marrying into your family on my worst enemy!'

'And just how do you propose to do it? By bullying and intimidation? I'm beginning to feel extremely sorry for Nicky, Miss Royle; I can well imagine what it must be like to be ruled by someone who's so completely taken up with her own ambitions that she has nothing left for any normal family feelings,' he finished bitingly.

'Why, you. . .! Get out of my office. You're the most odious, intolerant man I've ever known!' She picked up a paperweight ready to hurl it at him, but he stepped quickly forward and twisted her wrist until she had to let go and the paperweight dropped with a crash to the floor.

Alex Brandon's grey eyes glittered angrily down into her brown ones. 'That's another thing about liberated women—they always resort to violence when they can't beat a man any other way.' His lips curled sneeringly, then he let go of her wrist and turned on his heel to walk unhurriedly out of the office.

For a long moment Sara stared after him, rubbing her wrist where he had twisted it, then she sat down heavily in her chair, still glaring resentfully at the door. She looked down at the work on her desk, knowing she ought to finish it, but it had been a long, traumatic day and she suddenly felt overwhelmed by tiredness. That insufferable man had really got under her skin, making her lose her temper and react out of all proportion to the incident. Usually she had a tight hold on her emotions and forced herself to keep calm, whatever the provocation, and in her job she got plenty of that! But this Brandon man had touched on a raw spot when he jibed at her relationship with Nicky and she had reacted with a violence and anger that had surprised herself.

It must be because I'm tired, she thought dully. She crossed to the window and looked down at the street below; the pavements were mostly clear now, only a few late workers hurrying to the nearby tube station, and the traffic that built into a jam every night at five was reduced to an odd car that accelerated towards the main road. Glancing at her watch, Sara saw that it was nearly seven o'clock. She *must* finish the cosmetic portfolio tonight if she was to have the next morning off to take Nicky back to school. Guiltily she bent to her work and by giving it her undivided attention managed to finish it by seven-thirty. Quickly she locked the folio away in the office safe and gathered her belongings together, as usual shoving some more work in her briefcase to take with her. She was about to leave when she hesitated; Alex Brandon had said that Nicky was with her boy-friend—what was his name? Richard something. Perhaps she wouldn't be back at the flat yet.

Picking up the phone, Sara dialled her own number and listened while it rang.

'Hallo?' Nicky's rather breathless voice answered almost as she was about to give up. 'Is that you, Richard?'

'No, it's Sara. Have you just come in?'

'Oh. No, I was having a bath.' Nicky's voice suddenly became dull and resentful.

'Look, Nicky, I've finished here now and should be home in about twenty minutes. How about putting on a couple of steaks and then we can talk while we eat?'

'I've already had a meal, thank you,' Nicky answered like a polite little girl.

'Well, I'm starving, so you can talk to me while I eat, then. And Nicky, I'm sorry if I was a bit abrupt this morning, but I had a lot on my mind. We'll start again from the beginning when I get home, shall we?'

'There's really no point, is there? You've already decided that it's some silly teenage crush that we'll both grow out of. And I'm sure you've got much more important things to do than listen to me, so if you don't mind I think I'll go straight to bed.'

'Nicky, don't be so childish, we can at least. . . .'

But her sister had rung off and Sara was left holding a silent phone, her anger returning at this downright rudeness. Slamming down the receiver, she locked up the office and took the lift down to the basement, almost too tired and cross to remember to say her usual cheery goodnight to the attendant. The man looked after her as she accelerated away, shaking his head and wondering what had happened to upset one of his favourite customers.

Having given Nicky her key, Sara had to ring the doorbell of the flat and it was several minutes before her sister answered it. When she did, Sara saw that she was wearing one of her own new lace nightdresses with a matching negligee over the top, but as Nicky was about two sizes larger than Sara's slim figure the clothes were stretched at the seams.

Sara bit back the sharp remark she was going to make

and instead said in as mild a voice as she could, 'Didn't you bring any of your own clothes with you?'

'No, if the teachers had seen me carrying a bag they would have stopped me.'

'Just how did you get away?'

'I slipped out when we were supposed to be watching a hockey match,' Nicky admitted slowly.

'I see. Well, I phoned your headmistress and she was extremely put out. I had the devil of a job to convince her that you would behave for the rest of your stay there. It seems your work's been falling off rather a lot lately, too,' Sara added grimly as she put her briefcase down and started to take off her jacket.

'I put a steak on for you,' Nicky told her sulkily. 'It should be nearly ready now.'

'Thanks.' Sara crossed to the kitchen and began to prepare a tossed salad to go with the steak. 'Nicky, we have to talk this thing through. I don't want you to go back to school feeling unhappy and resentful. I haven't said that you can't marry, just that you're too young to contemplate it at the moment. After all, you're not eighteen until September.' She held up a hand as Nicky opened her mouth to speak. 'All right, I *know* you're going to say it's only a few months away, but you're still too young. Come and sit down and talk to me while I eat,' she coaxed.

But Nicky stood in the doorway and wouldn't come in. 'I'm awfully tired, I'd rather just go straight to bed. I expect you'll want to set out early tomorrow so you can get back to your precious job,' she added sullenly.

Sara turned to her in exasperation. 'My precious job, as you call it, has kept you at school and in clothes, holidays and pocket money for the last four years.'

Nicky's face paled. 'What do you mean?'

'I mean that your father didn't make any provision for your school fees in his will, so I paid them myself,' Sara told her bluntly.

Biting her lip, the younger girl suddenly looked ashamed. 'I'm sorry, I didn't know. I'll pay you back, of course, just as soon as I inherit Daddy's money,' she added stiffly.

Sara went to her and put her hands on her shoulders. 'Idiot, I don't want your money. I only told you because it's about time you opened your eyes a little. All I want is for you to have a good education so that you're already way up the ladder when you start your career—not have to fight your way up every rung like I did.' She looked hopefully into her sister's face, but Nicky wouldn't look her in the eyes. Exasperatedly Sara gave her a little shake. 'Anyway, you don't come into the money until you're twenty-five.'

'Unless I marry first,' Nicky reminded her defiantly.

'But not unless I give my blessing, and I certainly don't intend to do that until you've finished your education,' Sara retorted.

Nicky stared at her, her face white. 'You're mean and hateful! Just because no one has ever been in love with you, you don't want Richard to love me. And you care so much about money you can't see that it doesn't matter to us. Because we're going to get married anyway and there's nothing you can do to stop us!' Then she turned, tears running down her face, and ran into the spare bedroom, slamming the door behind her.

Sara took a hasty step to follow, but then stopped. What would be the use? In the mood Nicky was in at the moment she would never listen to reason. Sara sighed and turned back to the cooker. The steak was overdone and looked like a piece of leather. After one mouthful she pushed the plate aside; she didn't feel hungry now anyway. The nasty remarks that Nicky had shouted at her still rang in her ears. Was that really how the younger girl thought of her, as leading a loveless existence with making money her only driving force?

She picked up her cup of coffee and watched the steam rise from the surface. Was that the impression she gave? Slowly she tried to look at herself as others saw her. It was true that money was important to her —she knew very few people to whom it wasn't important! Money had been very tight after her own father died, and even when her mother had married again things hadn't been easy because her stepfather had been trying to start up his own business and every available penny had been put into building it up. There hadn't been enough for Sara's education and she had had to leave school at seventeen and get a job although she had desperately longed to go to university. It was only later that the business had begun to make a profit, and the really big money hadn't come until shortly before his death when the business became so successful that it had been taken over by a large company for a lump sum.

He had left everything in trust for Nicky, except for five thousand pounds for Sara, and this she had spent on the deposit for the flat, feeling that the most important thing was for Nicky to always have somewhere to call home, somewhere to come to during the holidays from school. It had been hard to pay off the mortgage and buy furniture out of her salary as well as pay the school fees, and even now, when the mortgage wasn't such a weight round her neck and she could afford the things Nicky's father hadn't had time to provide for his daughter, and even spare some money to spend on things for herself: books, china, an occasional painting; she still remembered with a shudder the times when it had been a hard struggle to even clothe herself decently. So perhaps money was a strong motivation, because she was darn sure that she was never going to be without it again, and that meant holding down her job until she was so good at it that she need never feel insecure.

And loveless? She smiled slightly until she remembered the other accusations that had been levelled at her that day. By Nicky and by Alex Brandon. Nicky had said that no one had ever loved her, but that wasn't true. Once, when she was only nineteen, she had fallen in love with a man only a year or two older than herself who worked in the same agency. He was a carefree, happy-go-lucky character who was great fun to be with. For a while the affair had been almost idyllic; they had got engaged and were constantly together although they knew they would have to wait to get married until they had saved enough for the deposit for a house. Often he took days off, using illness as an excuse, but they invariably coincided with Wimbledon or Lords. One day he persuaded Sara to do the same, but she had taken an important paper home the evening before and the agency sent someone round to collect it. The resulting row had almost cost her her job and had taught her a lesson she never forgot, making her work harder than ever to make up for it.

And then she had been promoted ahead of her fiancé. He had laughed at first, passing it off as just a fluke, only half-jokingly saying that she must have fluttered her eyelashes at the boss, but they both knew well enough that in advertising you only get promotion through merit, and something died in their relationship. Shortly after she received a second promotion he went out and spent their joint savings on a power-boat. Sara had known then that it was over. She went to a firm of head-hunters—the talent-spotting agencies in the advertising world—and they had immediately found her a job as a copywriter with another advertising firm. But it had hurt dreadfully that he wasn't man enough to take her success, and that she had had to be the one to make the move.

Since then she had made it a rule never to go out with anyone in the same line of business and, despite the accusations that Alex Brandon had levelled at her, there had been many men who had fallen for her attractive face and figure. Two or three of them had got serious enough to propose to her, but by then she had the financial worry of the flat and Nicky and she had honestly told them about it, not thinking it fair to burden them with her responsibilities. Or had she just used that as an excuse?

Sara refilled her coffee cup and wandered into the living-room, kicking off her shoes while she sat in an armchair and listened to a record. Over the last few years her job had become increasingly important to her. If something crucial cropped up she had no compunction in breaking a date so that she could deal with the problem, and this attitude had angered more than one man who thought that he should have come first. But Sara knew full well that if their situation had been reversed the man would have done the same thing and expected her to understand and accept it, so she had given their anger short shrift. They could accept her as she was, or—goodbye, it was fun while it lasted.

And perhaps it was this independent attitude that

put men off, because she hadn't had a steady boy-friend for some time, now that she came to think about it. In fact she tended to use work crises as a test to see how a man would react. If he stopped seeing her, then all well and good, he wasn't the man for her, and if he came back for more...? Sara hesitated, a frown between her eyes. Didn't she lose respect for a man if he let her walk over him too often? Restlessly she got up and went into the kitchen to do the washing-up, and afterwards sat at the kitchen table where she resolutely opened her case and took out the work she had brought home with her. All right, suppose she hadn't had a relationship of any length for some time, it didn't mean that she was never asked out. She had turned down two invitations only this month. And who needed a man permanently around anyway? She had a worthwhile job that stretched her undoubted talents and to which she devoted all her energy. A man would only get in the way. So damn Nicky and damn that impossible man Brandon! She'd got what she wanted out of life and if it didn't happen to coincide with the old-fashioned ideas of others, then it was just too bad!

It was late before Sara put her work away with a yawn, and she was asleep almost as her head touched the pillow, but she awoke suddenly, startlingly, the hairs at the back of her neck pricking with fright. She was completely alert, alive to every sound, just as our primitive ancestors must have been when they sensed danger.

'Nicky, is that you?' she called sharply, but there was no reply. Quickly she groped for the bedside lamp and switched it on, noting that it was three in the morning before she moved out into the still dark hallway. Switching the light on here too, Sara gently eased open the door of her sister's room. Nicky was fast asleep, she could just make out her fair hair on the pillow and the shape of her form huddled beneath the bedclothes. Quietly she shut the door and checked the rest of the flat before going back to bed, a little frown of puzzlement on her face. Must have been dreaming, she supposed, although she couldn't remember doing so. For a long time she lay awake, alert for any other sounds, but everything was still and eventually she drifted off to sleep again.

The sound of the phone ringing penetrated dimly to her ears later that morning and made her sit up with a jerk. Heavens, what time was it? On seeing that it was seven-thirty she almost leaped out of bed, wondering why on earth she hadn't heard the alarm. Then realisation hit her and she remembered she was taking Nicky back to school today and there was no need to panic. But the phone was still ringing shrilly and she hurried into the sitting-room to answer it.

'Yes, hallo. Who is it?' she asked, smothering a yawn.

'This is Alex Brandon,' a very wide-awake voice informed her tersely. 'Is your sister with you?'

'Nicky? Of course she is,' Sara answered in some astonishment.

'Are you sure?'

'Yes, I'm quite sure. Why on earth do you want to know?'

'Because Richard has done a bunk, and he's left a note saying that he's gone off with Nicky! I found it when I went in to wake him this morning. But if you say your sister is with you....' He paused. 'Miss Royle? Are you still there?'

'Yes—yes, I'm here,' Sara said very slowly, her hands gripping the receiver.

Alex Brandon's voice sharpened. 'Look, are you absolutely certain Nicky's there? Have you seen her this morning? You sound as if you've just got up yourself and. . . .'

Sara interrupted him: 'I—I think you'd better hold on.' She put down the receiver and went quickly to Nicky's room. It looked exactly the same as it had in the night, but now the dim light made the outline in the bed look unnatural. Hastily she pulled open the curtains and then stood still, bracing herself to pull back the covers. The hair was one of her own hairpieces and the body was a rolled-up blanket. There was a note pinned to the pillow. Feeling suddenly weak, Sara sat on the edge of the bed and opened it with trembling fingers. It was very short: 'I'm going away with Richard. We shall get married as soon as I'm eighteen. Please don't worry about me, Nicky.'

The idiot! The crazy little idiot! For a moment anger almost drove the fear from Sara's mind. Nicky with only some unknown boy to look after her. And that boy's uncle on the other end of the phone she remembered as she bit her lip.

'Hallo, Mr Brandon? Nicky's gone too,' she said baldly when she picked up the phone. 'She left a dummy in her bed to fool me.'

'And you very naturally fell for it,' Alex Brandon said with heavy sarcasm.

'When you've finished enjoying yourself at my expense, perhaps you could come back to the *slightly* more important matter of them running away together,' Sara retorted, fear for Nicky making her voice sharp.

'Their elopement you mean, don't you?'

'I don't suppose your nephew said where they were going?' Sara asked, ignoring his remark.

'Hardly. I know he hadn't much money on him, so presumably they're going to friends, but whichever way they're going they will probably have tried to hitch a lift. Are they likely to have gone to friends of Nicky's?'

'No, all her friends are at school,' Sara answered almost offhandedly, her mind racing as she tried to put herself in Nicky's place. 'Hasn't your nephew any relations he might have gone to? Grandparents or something?'

'No, but he does have friends at university who have digs outside the college. He'll probably try to move in with them for a while. I'm going to drive over to the college and see if I can find out anything there.' His voice was hard and decisive. 'Can you drive?'

'Yes, of course I can drive,' Sara answered tartly.

'Then I suggest you take your car and head for Nicky's school. Some of her friends there might know something. That's if you can spare the time from your job, of course,' he added sardonically.

Sara gritted her teeth angrily. 'As a matter of fact I can spare the time, but not to waste it by going all the way to Canterbury unnecessarily. You may think you're the Brain of Britain, Mr Brandon, but I happen to *know* where they're going!' And she slammed the receiver down with a triumphant thud.

## CHAPTER TWO

THE traffic heading north out of London was heavy and there were several frustrating traffic jams to be sat through before Sara turned on to the M1 motorway at last. She made good speed for a while but noticed that her petrol gauge needle was rather low so drove into the next service area, first pulling up outside the restaurant complex. Locking the car, she hurried through to the telephone booths, but they were all full and she had to wait, tapping her foot impatiently.

It seemed that she had been hurrying ever since the call from Alex Brandon. The telephone had rung twice more immediately after she had slammed the receiver down on him, but Sara had ignored it, imagining his anger with some satisfaction. After dressing and packing some clothes, she had driven to the office where she had left the work she had taken home and gone immediately to see the manager. She had baldly explained that a family problem had arisen and she would need at least a week's compassionate leave. If he wouldn't grant her the leave he could take it off her holidays, but she was taking the time off anyway. The poor man had looked startled at this arbitrary treatment from someone who was usually so accommodating and he hastened to assure her that she could have as much time as she wanted.

Sara had thanked him and gone back to her office to make a long-distance call. It was answered by a woman with a heavy northern accent. 'Yes, what do 'ee want?'

'Mrs Ogden? This is Sara Royle. How is Miss Quinlan? Is she up and about today?'

'Well, miss, she's not feeling all that bright this morning,' the woman's rather despondent voice informed her. 'Still, I expect she'll get up later, she usually does. Did you want to speak to her?'

'No, please don't disturb her. Look, I believe Nicky might turn up there with a friend. Probably today, but it could be tomorrow. If she does, don't say that I called, but make sure they stay with you until I can get up there, will you?' she asked anxiously.

There was a silence at the other end of the line, until Mrs Ogden said slowly, 'A bit of trouble, is there?'

'Yes, I'm afraid so. You will try and keep her there, won't you?'

'Don't you worry, Miss Sara. She'll stay, I'll make sure of that.'

After thanking her, Sara had got in her car and started off for Cumbria, crossing her fingers that she was right and that Nicky had gone to take refuge with her godmother, Veronica Quinlan, who was a semi-invalid and lived quietly with her devoted housekeeper and nurse, Mrs Ogden, in an old, rather remote house overlooking one of the smaller lakes.

A phone booth was free at last and now the housekeeper answered again, telling her that there had been no sign of the runaways as yet, nor any telephone call to say they were on their way. The news didn't depress Sara too much; it was really too soon for them to have managed to get that far yet and they were probably too hard up to waste money on an unnecessary phone call; they were probably standing at the roadside somewhere along the way trying to hitch a lift. This thought made her want to hurry to try to catch up with them and she stepped quickly out of the booth. A man who had been leaning negligently against the wall, arms folded, while he waited, straightened up as she came out and moved to block her way. It was Alex Brandon.

Sara stopped and stared up at him in astonishment. 'You? But I thought you were. . . .'

'Scouring the college? What was the point in going there when you were so obliging as to tell me that you knew where they were heading?'

'How did you know which way to go?' Sara asked suspiciously.

'Simple,' he said lazily. 'I drove over to your flat and waited for you to come out, then I followed you.'

Sara glared at him. 'You've got a nerve! I thought you were going to talk to your nephew and persuade him to wait? If you ask me he's completely irresponsible and no more fit to be married than you are to look after him, and. . . .'

'But I didn't ask you. And if it comes to that you're no more fit to be guardian of a silly, romantic schoolgirl, so let's just stop abusing one another and make up our minds what we're going to do about the situation, shall we?' he cut in sharply.

'You can do what you like. I'm going to find Nicky and take her back to school before this—this whole stupid episode gets out of proportion.'

'And Richard?'

'He's your problem, not mine.' Sara went to walk past him, but he put out his hand and caught her arm, effectively stopping her.

'Not so fast, Miss Royle. I'm not going to let you leave Richard stranded high and dry somewhere while you drag your sister back to school,' he said angrily. Then less heatedly, 'Look, we both want the same thing, so why don't we talk this over while we have a cup of coffee? A quarter of an hour isn't going to make any difference,' he added, seeing Sara about to shake her head. 'And it would help if we could agree on our future attitude and actions before we found them, don't you think?'

While he was speaking he had been leading her inexorably towards the coffee shop. Sara had tried to pull her arm away, but he held her so firmly that she would have had to resort to an undignified struggle to get free.

'And you said it was only women who resorted to violence when they couldn't get their own way,' she remarked caustically when they were finally seated at a table, rubbing her arm where his fingers had gripped her to emphasise her point.

'That wasn't violence—I was merely helping you along,' he replied coolly.

'Like hell! I would have had to scream the place down before you'd let go.'

'Not even then. I'd merely have told any interested spectators that you were suffering from a mild breakdown due to the strain of overwork, and have taken you somewhere where you could have screamed your head off in private,' he told her, a gleam of malicious amusement in his grey eyes.

'Do you always deal so arbitrarily with anyone who crosses you?' Sara demanded.

'Only with the more foolish members of your sex.'

Derisively Sara said, 'I bet your wife just loves that.'

'I'm not married, but if I were it wouldn't be to the type of female who makes unnecessary scenes in public,' he replied bitingly. 'Drink your coffee.'

'I'll drink it when I'm good and ready,' she answered defiantly.

Alex Brandon shrugged. 'Suit yourself.' He poured cream into his own cup. Today he wasn't wearing his dark city suit, but instead a cream polo-neck sweater with tan cord trousers and a matching loose jacket. The more casual clothes didn't soften his appearance any, though; if anything they emphasised his height and the width of his shoulders. And his face was as hard and implacable as ever.

He glanced up and caught her watching him. Raising a mocking eyebrow, he said, 'Shall we get down to business? Exactly where do you think they're heading? And what makes you so sure?'

Sara bent to drink her own coffee as she wondered whether or not to tell him. She would much prefer to talk with Nicky and her boy-friend alone, without Alex Brandon butting in, so that she could make up her mind what to do. She felt guilty about not having insisted that Nicky talk the matter out the night before instead of letting her go off to bed, and she wanted time now to talk to both of them, to decide whether this was just a schoolgirl crush or what could be a lasting relationship. If it was the former she would have to tread very carefully, causing as little hurt as possible, but not making any untruthful promises for the future just to ease the situation and make it less painful for Nicky now. And if she did think it was serious her task would be even harder. But for Nicky's sake she would have to try and split them up for now, probably by taking the boy aside and appealing to his better nature. And she couldn't do that with Alex Brandon breathing down her neck!

She lifted her head and found that he was watching her as closely as she had looked at him earlier. 'Nicky has a godmother who lives in the north. She's been there several times for holidays in the last few years and I'm pretty sure that's where she'd go.'

'Where in the north?' came the inevitable question.

Squaring her shoulders, Sara looked at him steadily. 'I'm not going to tell you. I want the chance to talk to Nicky alone. But if you like you can wait in a hotel in Manchester and I'll drop your Richard off there on the way back south.'

His jaw tightened. 'After you've given him a verbal lashing that will make him feel like a guilty criminal and completely destroy his confidence, I suppose?'

'I have no intention of giving him a talking to—not that he doesn't seem to stand in crying need of one,' she retorted. 'I just want to....'

'Don't worry, I'm not going to give you the chance. I'm coming with you, even if I have to follow you all the way to Scotland!'

'That's ridiculous! You couldn't possibly follow me to—all that way. I could lose you easily.'

'You could try,' he retorted sardonically. 'But I agree that it's ridiculous, so why don't we take it as read that I'm coming along and travel together? You can leave your car here and we'll take mine.'

Sara gave a little disbelieving laugh. 'You really expect me to agree to that? I wouldn't put it past you to dump me somewhere the moment you found out where they were going.'

Alex Brandon looked at her derisively. 'What a strange type of man you must mix with,' he remarked with heavy sarcasm. 'Do all your boy-friends kick you out of their cars when, or if, you don't play ball?'

Her fingers tightened on her coffee cup and it took a great deal of resolve not to throw the contents in his face. 'According to you, I don't have any boy-friends,' she reminded him tartly.

With acid irony, he said, 'But there is one class of man—if you can call them that—who're perverted enough to go for your type. I think they call them mascochists.'

Eyes ablaze with anger, Sara crashed down her cup and headed out of the coffee shop, but she hadn't gone ten yards before he was by her side. Furiously she turned on him. 'Keep away from me, d'you hear me? And don't try to follow me, because if you do I'll call the police. And see how you get out of that one!'

Still seething, she hurried away from him and walked across to her car, driving it round to the petrol pumps. While she was there she asked the attendant if he had seen a boy and a girl trying to hitch a lift earlier that day.

When she described Nicky, the man rubbed his chin and said, 'I seem to remember a couple of kids, very early this morning it was. I think they got a lift on a container van, but I'm not sure. Look, miss, why don't you go over to the commercial section? The chap on the diesel pumps over there would be able to tell you better than I can. You can leave your car here for a minute, it isn't in the way.'

Sara thanked him and strode briskly across the garage area to where the commercial vehicles were being filled up. She had to wait for a while before the attendant was free to talk to her, but he immediately recognised her description and told her that Nicky and Richard had got a lift on a lorry that was going up the motorway as far as Rugby. The news brought her heartfelt relief; it meant that she had been right in her guess that they were making for the Lake District. And they would have to leave the M1 at Rugby so that they could try to get a lift going towards the M6 via Birmingham, she realised. With a lighter step she hurried back to the garage and to her surprise found the attendant bending over her car. He straightened as she approached and turned towards her, his face red with anger.

'I've never seen nothing like it!' he said, his voice outraged. 'Just backed in and smashed straight into it, he did, and then drove away fast before I could even switch off the pump. He must've known he'd done it, though why a van should be backing in 'ere, I don't know.'

'Done it? Done what?' He stepped aside and Sara gave a gasp of incredulous dismay. 'Oh, no!' The front of her car had been smashed in like a trodden can. The lights were broken in the crumpled wings, water trickled from the perforated radiator, and the bent bumper trailed on the ground. 'What happened? Who did it?' For a distracted moment she had the wild idea that Alex Brandon had been responsible, but the attendant soon enlightened her.

'It was a big van. Didn't have a name on the side, or I'd have seen it, and the number plate was too dirty to read. I'm sorry, miss, I really am.'

'It's all right, it's not your fault. But lord, what a mess!'

Another car drew up at the pumps and the man went away to serve while Sara took a closer look at the damage. She gave a sigh of vexation. She wasn't going any further in that today, that was for sure.

A languid voice behind her said, 'Having a spot of trouble?'

Sara squared her shoulders and turned; she rather thought she'd recognise that voice anywhere now. 'Someone backed into my car,' she told Alex Brandon.

She watched his face carefully, ready to let fly at the slightest hint of amusement or triumph, but his features were completely enigmatical as he, too, examined the damage. 'Hm. I'm afraid that's going to take some time to repair,' he remarked as he looked back at her. 'What are you going to do?'

Her eyes challenged his as she said coldly, 'I'm going to leave this here and hire another one, of course.'

But he merely nodded and sauntered back to his own vehicle. Sara gazed at his broad back for a moment, slightly baffled by his nonchalance. Then she shrugged it off and went over to the repair section to make arrangements for the car to be mended, then over to yet another office to hire a car. Twenty minutes later she walked back to the petrol pumps, more slowly this time.

Alex Brandon was still there, parked out of the way of the other vehicles, leaning against his car and smoking a cigarette. With a stab of pure envy, Sara saw that he had a silver-grey Aston Martin that couldn't have cost a penny under ten thousand pounds. He straightened as she walked reluctantly towards him, and ground out his cigarette.

'Why are you still here?' she demanded as she began to take her belongings from her car.

'Have you forgotten? I'm supposed to be following you. Where's the new car?'

'I couldn't get one,' she admitted reluctantly. 'It seems the men who service them are on strike and there won't be any available until tomorrow.'

He raised an eyebrow. 'So?'

'So I'll try and get a lift,' she retorted as she lugged her case out of the boot and slammed it shut.

Shaking his head in reproof, Alex Brandon said in a remonstrating voice, 'Hasn't anybody ever told you not to take lifts from strange men? Anything might happen—before you have a chance to demonstrate what type of woman you are, that is.'

'*You* offered me a lift and there aren't many men stranger than you,' she flashed back.

'But at least you know me.'

'You mean, better the devil you know than the devil you don't.'

'And you know that I wouldn't touch you with a barge pole,' he added with a definitely malicious note in his tone.

Sara glared at him, wishing him everything under the sun, but her glance went past him to the sleek lines of that lovely, lovely car. 'All right,' she said ungraciously, 'I'll come with you.'

'Please, Alex.'

'What?'

'Say, please, Alex,' he commanded laconically.

Her temper overflowing at that, Sara yelled at him, 'Why the hell should I? If it hadn't been for your scheming nephew I wouldn't be chasing all over the country like this. And if you think I'm going to grovel to you, you're crazy! I'd rather get a lift from the randiest lorry driver on the motorway than go with you. You're the most arrogant, conceited....' But her words were lost as he started to get in his car and shut the door. 'Oh, hell!' Sara stamped her foot on the ground and clenched her teeth. 'Oh, all right. Please, please, please! There—does that satisfy you?'

'Alex,' he insisted.

She snorted, then snapped out, 'Alex.'

'It could have been said with better grace, but I suppose that's the best one can hope for coming from a termagant like you.' He came round and opened the boot to put her case in and she noticed that he, too, had brought an overnight bag.

Still smarting with humiliation, Sara got into the passenger seat of the sumptuous sports car.

'Fasten your seat belt,' he ordered as he pulled away.

'Why? Are you such a bad driver?'

He stopped the car. 'Look, let's get one thing straight from the beginning, shall we?' he said tersely, a contemptuous look in his hard grey eyes. 'I don't like having to be thrown in your company any more than you like being in mine, but if we have to be together then for God's sake let's stop this everlasting bickering and behave like rational human beings. I don't know how you get your kicks, but personally I don't see any point in being at each other's throats all the time. We both want the same thing in the long run, which is the best for our respective charges with the least hurt and unhappiness, so let's try and call a truce, or bury the hatchet, or whatever cliché seems to fit, until all this is over, shall we?'

Sara looked at him for long seconds as he sat so close beside her, his arm touching her own. He was looking at her steadily, one eyebrow raised in interrogation. Sitting back with a sigh, she said flatly, 'Yes, I suppose so,' and began to fasten her safety strap.

He started off again and when they were back on the motorway and zipping up the outside lane, Sara said rather stiffly, 'I'm sorry if I shouted at you back there; I was rather upset about my car.'

After giving her a quick glance, he said, 'Is it your own?'

'No, it's the company's thank goodness, but they're bound to be annoyed that I didn't get the van driver's number.'

His voice devoid of expression, he said, 'I shouldn't worry, it happens all the time.' He paused. 'Do we stay on the motorway all the way?'

'Oh, no, we turn off on to the M6. But I talked to a garage attendant who said he saw a girl like Nicky travelling with a boy, and they got a lift as far as Rugby, so perhaps we ought to stop there and ask again.'

'Okay. Put the radio or cassette player on if you want some music.'

'It won't disturb you?'

He shook his head. 'No.'

Sara selected a cassette and inserted it in the player and for some time they drove without speaking. He drove well, she noticed; his strong hands holding the wheel of the powerful car under iron control, driving up to the limit and flashing past the slower cars, but never taking any chances, always having mastery of the road. At length he said, 'I've left my cigarettes in my jacket. Get them for me, please, would you, Sara?'

So they were to be on first name terms, were they? 'Have one of mine,' she said deliberately, taking a packet from her bag. 'And you must let me know the cost of the petrol so that I can go halves with you.' She pressed in the lighter on the dashboard and then passed the lit cigarette to him.

As he took it from her she had the impression that his lips twitched in amusement, but he merely said, 'Of course,' and pulled on the cigarette.

At the service area before the turn-off for the M6, they both got out, Sara to check that the runaways weren't by some chance still in the coffee shop, Alex to question the garage attendants to see if he could find out anything.

'They got a lift all right, but the chap didn't know how far it was going. He said he thought he remembered Stoke-on-Trent on the side of the lorry, but he couldn't be sure,' Alex told her when he came back to the car. 'Look, don't you think it's about time you told me where they're headed? I promise not to leave you stranded if you do,' he added with a wry twist to his mouth.

Sara flushed slightly. 'Nicky's godmother, Veronica Quinlan, lives in the Lake District. The nearest town of any size is Keswick.'

'Keswick.' He picked up a road atlas. 'The M6 goes nearly all the way.' After glancing at his watch, he began, 'I think we'd better have....' then paused. 'Or rather, I *suggest* we have lunch now and then push on until we find them. How does that suit you?'

Sara looked at him for a moment and then, to Alex's surprise, she laughed, her brown eyes dancing with amusement. 'It suits me fine.'

She went to get out of the car again, but he put out a hand to stop her, an arrested expression in his eyes. 'What's so funny?'

The laughter still in her face, she replied, 'You, trying to make allowances for Women's Lib. Are you always so autocratic?'

'Most women seem to like the masterful type.'

Sara wrinkled her nose. 'Not women—doormats.'

After a light lunch they headed north again.

'We have a choice of heading straight for Nicky's godmother's and waiting for them there, or of looking for them on the way,' Alex remarked. 'At least we know that they're on this road, but if they're travelling in a lorry we could quite easily overtake them.'

'Yes, I know. I suppose the sensible thing would be to go straight there, but I hate to think of them being stuck somewhere trying to get a lift when we're so near.'

'Mm. Tell you what, we're going to have to stop for

petrol somewhere along the road anyway, so why don't we head for Stoke and ask again there? If we hear nothing of them, then we'll head for the Lake District.'

Sara readily agreed and they went on with a more relaxed atmosphere between them. Presently she said, 'This is a beautiful car. Is it your own?'

'Sort of. It's officially down as belonging to the company, but as I own the company I suppose that makes it mine.'

'What kind of work do you do?'

He overtook a noisy juggernaut before replying, 'It's a software firm. In other words I sell brainpower. When large organisations want to go over to computers they need a team of experts to advise them on programming; I gather together the right men with the right experience and send them along.'

'I'm impressed,' Sara remarked truthfully, knowing just how complex the computer world could be.

'Don't be. It's just something I happen to be trained to do, and I was lucky enough to have some capital left to me so that I could start the firm. I don't go on field work myself much now, unless it's a very important job—computerising the New York stock exchange or something—otherwise I just stay home and organise. How about you? How did you get into your job?'

Sara shrugged slightly. 'By the back door. I started out as a secretary and only began doing copywriting when someone was away ill and they were stuck for staff. Then I went to evening classes and took the CAM certificate.'

'CAM?'

'Sorry, it stands for Communication, Advertising and Marketing. After that I progressed gradually up the ladder and I'm now an account director—that's a person who liaises between the agency and the advertiser clients.'

'Sounds as if you might have to be a bit of a diplomat.'

'It can be a very fraught role, trying to keep the customer happy and sort out the aggro,' she admitted, remembering more than one prickly customer who always made trouble. 'But it's fun too, because you have an enormous range of people working within the agency, all with different skills and personalities, and you have to dovetail them together, form them into a team, as well as co-ordinate all the agency services: market research, media planning and production.' She stopped, aware that she was running on. 'But I'm sure you don't want a lecture on the joys of advertising.'

'You make it sound interesting. I've always imagined it to be a rather cut-throat industry where everyone sat around either drawing cartoon characters or making up jingles and slogans all day.'

With a rather twisted smile, Sara said, 'Most people do tend to think that way, and a lot of that kind of thing does come into it, but it's a very small part in relation to the whole. Don't you use advertising in your company?'

Alex shook his head. 'Never needed to. We've always been recommended by satisfied customers so far.' He paused, then, 'You're very keen on your work.' It was a statement, not a question.

'I have to be, it's my living. We don't all have rich relations who leave us enough to be independent, Mr Brandon.' There was a distinct note of bitterness in Sara's voice.

He shot her a glance. 'No, we don't, which is why it's up to the people who do to provide employment for those less fortunate, so that we all get a slice of the cake,' he replied evenly. Then, when she didn't answer, 'But you said that your sister was an heiress, didn't you?'

'Yes, her father—my stepfather—left the money in trust for her. It's to be hers when she's twenty-five, or before that if she marries with my blessing.'

'I see.'

'Do you?'

'Oh, yes, I think so. It explains why you're so against Nicky marrying, of course, and also why you're so bitter about inherited cash.'

Sara turned to glare at him. 'That's a rotten thing to say! I don't envy Nicky her money. I just don't want to see her waste it—that and her life.'

'It's her life and her money. What right have you got to dictate to her how she should spend either?'

Sitting back in her seat, Sara stared fixedly ahead. 'You wouldn't understand even if I told you.'

'Try me.'

Taking the packet from her bag, she said, 'Do you want another cigarette?' and when he nodded, lit them up. 'How much further is it to Stoke?' she asked when she'd passed one to him.

'Changing the subject, Sara?' he asked quietly.

'I should have thought that was obvious to the meanest intelligence, let alone to a computer expert.'

'Why don't you want to talk about it?'

'Because my life is none of your business. We just happen to have the same interests at the moment, but that's as far as it goes. You keep out of my affairs and I'll more than willingly keep out of yours, Mr Brandon,' she remarked caustically.

'Alex,' he reminded her, apparently unperturbed by

her outburst. 'And I agree with you, your *affairs*,' he stressed the word, 'are your own concern.'

Sara got his meaning immediately and stared at him angrily. Of all the insufferable men to have got mixed up with! She could only wish fervently that they would soon catch up with Nicky and get the whole thing sorted out, because if she never had to see Alex Brandon again, it would be far too soon!

# CHAPTER THREE

It was at Stoke that they ran into a snag because at first they were unable to find any trace of the young people, but then Sara had the idea of asking the cashier at the pay desk in the coffee shop. When she met Alex in the entrance she was wearing a puzzled frown.

'What does your Richard look like?' she asked him.

'Richard? Oh, he's about five feet ten, rather thin with longish brown hair and spectacles. Why?'

Sara arched her brows in surprise. 'He's not like you then?'

'No, not particularly.'

'He doesn't sound very prepossessing,' she remarked without thinking.

'Well, your Nicky is hardly a new Brigitte Bardot,' he answered drily. 'Why do you want to know?'

'The woman at the cash desk said she remembered a young couple who came in only an hour or so ago, just after she came on duty. She was a bit vague on the description, but she definitely remembered the boy had glasses. She said they asked round for a lift and got one with a van driver who was just leaving. But the odd part is that they asked for a lift to Buxton. That isn't even on the M6, is it?'

Alex frowned. 'No, it's not. Let's go back to the car and look at the map.'

They did so and he had to switch on the courtesy light, the grey skies of the April afternoon becoming even darker as the first few spots of rain began to fall.

'Buxton. Here it is, almost on the edge of the Peak District. Now why on earth should they be making for there?'

'Does Richard know anyone who lives in that area?'

'Not that I know of, although he did go there on a climbing holiday only last year. Perhaps he knows somewhere where he can hole up.' Alex looked at the map a moment longer, then made up his mind. 'Okay, we'll follow them. With any luck we might pick them up in Buxton. It can't be that big a place.'

But the town, that had once been an inland spa, was bigger than they expected and they had to enquire at several places before Alex struck lucky at a transport café. He came hurrying back to the car, his collar up against the now heavy downpour. 'Edale,' he said as he got back in. 'The van driver dropped them off here and they used the proprietor's phone to order a taxi to take them to Edale. Seems it's quite popular because it's the start of a walk across the Pennines.'

He started the engine and the powerful beams of the headlights cut through the driving rain as they headed up the high slopes of the hills. Sara didn't talk much other than to give him directions when necessary, letting him concentrate on tackling the tricky bends which would have required all his attention in the best of conditions. By the time they pulled up in the centre of Edale it was pitch dark.

Looking across the street at the lights of a stone-built hotel, Alex said rather exasperatedly, 'Better try there first, I suppose, although it looks beyond Richard's means. Still, they might be able to give us some help about other accommodation.' He turned to Sara. 'There's no point in us both chasing around and getting wet. Why don't you stay in the bar at the hotel until I find them?'

'I'd rather come along, thanks,' Sara said rather tightly.

The exasperation in his voice increased. 'Look, I promise I'll come back for you before I talk to them. Anyway, I'm not about to blow my top if we do find them.'

'Aren't you?' Sara asked drily. 'You haven't struck me as being the particularly reticent type when it comes to handing out insults and sarcastic remarks, so if you don't mind, I'll come along.'

'And if I do mind?'

'I'm still coming. Nicky will probably be in a highly emotional state as it is, and I don't want you upsetting her more. She can be quite impossible to handle if she gets hysterical.'

'Oh, I see. You're merely thinking of the difficulties *you* might have to put up with. I should have known,' he remarked, his voice heavy with irony.

'Of course you should,' Sara returned sweetly. 'Why else would I submit myself to another minute of your charming company except for that reason? Now are you going to enquire, or would you rather I did it for you?'

Alex gave a rather crooked grin, got out of the warm interior of the car and sprinted across to the hotel. Within ten minutes he was back, but had only a list of local places they could try.

'The receptionist sold me a local map so we should be able to find them easily enough. Here, you'd better mark the places on the map and we'll go to the nearest first.'

'*What* a good idea,' Sara commented admiringly. 'How *terribly* clever of you to think of it. I'm sure I'd *never* have been able to think of anything as brilliant as that!'

She bent to look at the list, but his hand came out to cup her chin as he turned her round to face him. 'Sara.' His voice was soft as silk, but there was also a distinct hint of steel behind it. 'Just watch it, will you?'

It took them nearly two hours to cover all the places on the list, several of them being outside the sprawling village, and in all of them they had drawn a blank.

'But they must be somewhere,' Sara said worriedly. 'They can't have just disappeared.'

'They must be staying at a private house with someone we don't know about. It's the only explanation,' Alex said irritably. 'And short of knocking on every door in the place there's no way we're going to find them. We'll have to go back to the village centre now anyway, so that I can fill up with petrol again before the garage shuts.'

He reversed and turned, the wheels sending up showers of mud from the verge. The inside of the car felt cold and dank now. Alex's jacket was soaked on the shoulders and his dark hair clung wetly to his forehead. As they drove back, Sara said slowly, 'That transport café at Buxton—it was called Pete's Pull-in, wasn't it?'

'Possibly. I didn't particularly notice. Why do you ask?'

'Well, if they phoned for a taxi from there, the proprietor could give us the number too, and we could. . . .'

'Phone the taxi service and find out what address the driver took them to,' Alex finished for her. 'Sara, that was *almost* worth bringing you along for.'

Before long they were back at the hotel where Sara

had a much-needed drink in the bar while Alex used the phone.

'No wonder we couldn't find them,' he remarked as he joined her. 'The taxi took them to an empty cottage. They got the key from the next door neighbour, evidently. I wonder how the dickens they knew about it, though.' He pushed the damp hair back from his forehead. 'Is this drink for me?'

'Yes, I ordered you a Glenfiddich. You looked the malt whisky type.'

He looked at her and grinned wryly. 'I suppose you get used to summing up people when you're in your line of business?'

'Of course. And the drink's already paid for,' she added as he took out his wallet.

'Of course.' He put it back in his pocket and looked at her over the glass. 'Cheers. I've never had a woman buy me a drink before.'

Sara gave a mirthless smile. 'Unfortunately it won't choke you.'

And then he laughed, a full masculine laugh that completely transformed his features, giving him a younger, carefree look.

Staring at him in alarm, Sara said in mock concern, 'You know, Mr Brandon, you really should be careful. If you laugh too often people might begin to think you were almost human. And now I think we'd better go and find our lost sheep, don't you?'

'I suppose you're right,' He put down his glass with something like reluctance, and Sara didn't blame him —she wasn't looking forward to the next hour herself.

They found the cottage easily enough. 'We must have passed it about three times,' Alex remarked ruefully as they pulled up outside.

'It's all in darkness,' Sara said as she peered through the rain-splashed window. 'You don't think they've gone to...?' she stopped hurriedly.

'Lord, I hope not,' Alex said fervently. 'But they might be in the back. I'll go and rouse them.'

'I'm coming with you.' Sara hopped out of the car and ran to stand beside him under the shelter of the porch, the rain beating noisily down. Alex picked up the knocker and banged it hard. At first there was no response, so he knocked harder and longer. A sash window above them was pushed up squeakily and a man leant out.

'Who the hell's that?'

'Richard, is that you?'

'No, it damn well isn't.'

The man went to slam down the window, but Alex stepped out to look at him. 'Wait. Is Richard French staying with you?'

'No, he isn't, and if you don't clear off I'll throw a bucket of water at you!'

'It wouldn't make me any wetter than I am already, and I'm not leaving until I'm sure the person I'm looking for isn't here.'

There was a string of swearwords from above them and after a few minutes the door was swung open with a thud. The youth who stood before them with only a cheap dressing-gown covering him was tall and thin with long brown hair and Elton John spectacles, but one glance at Alex's tight face told her that it wasn't Richard.

'All right,' the youth exploded. 'If you don't believe me then come and look for yourself. What are you, the police or something?'

Alex stepped hastily past him and glanced into the

ground floor rooms of the tiny place before hurrying up
the stairs.

'Can't even go on holiday without you police pigs
spoiling everything for us,' the youth said bitterly. He
looked at Sara who was still standing transfixed on the
doorstep. 'Is he a pig?'

'Oh, yes, definitely, but not the kind you mean.'

There came a girlish scream from above them and
Alex reappeared and ran hastily down the stairs. 'I'm
terribly sorry. I'm afraid we were given the wrong information. Here, please take this to make up for the
trouble and buy yourself a bottle of champagne or
something.' He caught hold of Sara's arm and bundled
her into the car, the youth still shouting names at them.

He started up the car and it shot forward with a
screech of tyres. 'My God, did you hear what he called
me, the little...?' he said through gritted teeth. 'Not
that he didn't have a perfect right after we'd barged in
on him like that. He had a girl up there too,' he added
savagely. 'She looked a bit like Nicky, I suppose, but
anyone with half an eye could have seen that they were
just hippies. Lord, I've never been so embarrassed in
my life as when I pushed open the door of that bedroom. She hadn't even bothered to....' he hastily bit
off what he was about to say. For a moment he was
silent, then said suspiciously, 'Sara?'

With great difficulty she answered, 'Yes, Alex?'

'Sara, are you...?'

But she couldn't contain herself any longer and gave
a stifled gurgle of laughter. She tried to stop but
couldn't and leaned back against the seat shaking with
uncontrollable mirth, helpless with it.

Alex braked to a stop and turned to glare at her
angrily. 'Stop that! I can't see anything at all funny in
what happened back there.'

Sara tried to point towards him but was still shaking so much that she could hardly raise her hand. 'You should have seen your face! You were furious.'

'And I still am. Sara, will you please stop?' He took hold of her shoulders and shook her none too gently. 'Now will you stop it? You have an extremely warped sense of humour,' he said nastily, and added, 'Do you realise we still haven't found them? If you hadn't been so quick to pick up the lead that woman in Stoke gave you we wouldn't have wasted all these hours on this wild goose chase.'

'Me?' Sara straightened up, her laughter sunk beneath indignation. 'Who was it who went into the transport café at Buxton and every guest house in Edale? Why didn't you check that it was the right couple if you're so clever?'

'Because after that first wrong piece of information I only had to ask if they'd seen a young couple, not give a detailed description,' he retorted bitingly. 'It was you who was so darn eager to catch them that you didn't check properly in the first place. By now they're probably sitting in front of a blazing fire at this Miss Quinlan's house in the Lake District. While we, thanks to you, are sitting in a cold car in the middle of a rainstorm, miles away from anywhere.'

Sara opened her mouth to argue angrily with him, but then saw a drop of water trickle from his hair and run down the side of his lean cheek and across the firm line of his jaw to land on the wet collar of his jacket. Instead she said mildly, 'So why are we sitting here arguing? The sooner we get going, the sooner we can get warm in front of that fire, too.'

There was a surprised look in Alex's eyes for a moment, then he nodded. 'All right, let's do that. I think if we keep along this road we should be able to eventually cut back on the M6 further up. You can navigate.'

He started off again, and with some difficulty in the swaying car, Sara picked out the quickest route. 'There's a turn to the left in about half a mile,' she told him. 'If we take that it should bring us out on the main road leading directly to the motorway.'

Alex grunted acknowledgement and concentrated on steering the high-powered car along the steeply climbing narrow roads, the windscreen wipers at maximum speed as they worked to clear a field of vision through the driving rain. He put his foot hard on the brake to take a sharp turn and Sara was thrown against the side of the car, the map light she was holding falling off her lap. Bending down, she groped to retrieve it, but had to unfasten her safety strap in order to reach down to where it had rolled right to the front of the car near her feet.

Alex glanced across at her. 'All right?'

'Yes, thanks.'

Finding it, she sat up again and opened the map book to find her place. Staring ahead through the darkness, she began to feel a growing unease as the car sped on through the night without the harsh beams of the headlights illuminating the turning they wanted. It had to be along here shortly, it must be.

As if reading her thoughts, Alex said, 'How far did you say that turning was?'

'About half a mile. We should have come to it before this.'

'Perhaps you misread the map?' he suggested.

Sara shot him a dark look but nevertheless bent to check. 'No,' she said positively. 'We must have passed it. We'd better turn back.'

'We'll go on for another mile or so just in case.'

Her voice rising, Sara said, 'What's the point of doing that if we've missed the turning? You're only wasting more time. Stop and turn round, I tell you.'

Alex glared at her. 'Are you sure you're looking at the right page of the map?' he asked, his voice heavy with sarcasm.

Stung, Sara retorted, 'Yes, I am. We must have passed the turning when I dropped the torch. And if you hadn't been driving so fast that the car swayed I wouldn't have dropped it in the first place.'

'Trust you to blame your inefficiency on someone else,' Alex said sneeringly. He braked and started to turn the long car in the narrow road, the back wheels going on to the grass verge as he did so. 'I bet if anything goes wrong in your job you make darn sure that some other poor devil gets the blame for it so that you don't have to carry the can.' He changed gear and began to reverse again, putting his arm along the back of the seat and turning his body towards her so that he could look out of the rear window where the reversing lights lit up the terrain.

'Of all the nerve!' Enraged beyond endurance by his acid and quite untrue remark, Sara lifted her hand and slapped him across the face.

Startled more than hurt, Alex turned his head to stare at her in shocked surprise. His face hardened and he began to say something, but then the back of the car started to fall sickeningly away beneath them and Sara found herself pitching forward against him as the side of the car rolled over to where the floor used to be.

She gave a cry of horror and fear, but then the car rocked a little and was still. The engine had stalled and for long seconds they were both silent with shock. Her heart pounding with fear, Sara was too stunned to move. Then Alex's voice, almost in her ear, said sharply, 'Sara, are you all right?'

'Yes. Yes, I think so.' She tried to move and found that she was held fast in his arms, lying on top of him. As she turned her head, his face touched hers. 'Are you?'

'Yes. Look, we'll have to try and get out of your door. Do you think you can pull yourself up and open it?'

'I'll try.' She began to turn away from him and his hands came round her waist, helping her. By putting one hand on the steering wheel and the other on the back of the seat, she managed to pull herself towards the door which was now where the roof should have been. Moving to get a better purchase on the handle, she heard a grunt below her. 'What's the matter?'

'You merely trod on me,' Alex said patiently. He lowered his hands a few inches down her hips and supported her while she opened the door and stood up. Then she hoisted herself up and swung her legs out, pushing away from the car to jump down on the ground.

Immediately the rain began to soak into the jacket of the trouser suit she was wearing and she was already very wet by the time Alex scrambled down beside her.

Quickly he went to examine the damage, then came back to her. 'God, what a mess! It's well and truly stuck in a ditch. Still, I suppose we were lucky; for one awful minute I thought we were going right down the side of the hill.' He went to the boot and pulled it open. 'There should be an umbrella in here somewhere. Here, Sara, take this and shelter under it while I fish for the map and the torch and find out where we are.' He opened the big black businessman's umbrella and thrust it towards her. 'Here, take it,' he said again.

She just stood there, making no attempt to move. Suddenly Alex was beside her, his voice urgent. 'It's all right, Sara, it's over. You're quite safe now.'

Alex went on talking to her, reassuring her, and slowly her trembling stilled and she was able to say shakily, 'I'm sorry. I've—I've never been in an accident before. It shook me—falling like that.' She found that she was clinging to the lapels of his jacket and that Alex again had his arm round her as they stood beneath the shelter of the umbrella. Hastily she disengaged herself.

'Serves you right,' he said unsympathetically. 'You should have put your safety strap back on. Now hold this while I get our things out of the car.'

He left her standing under the umbrella, the rain pattering noisily down on to it, her legs getting steadily wetter. Hopefully she looked around her, but the night was pitch dark; there was no sign of life anywhere, no lights, nothing. When Alex came back he was carrying their cases and a winter coat she had put in the boot. 'Here, you'd better put this on,' he ordered, taking the umbrella from her.

As he switched on the torch and studied the map, Sara noticed that he, too, had put on a heavy, belted trench coat. 'No point in going back to Edale,' he said after a moment. 'It will be quicker to go on in the direction we were heading and hope that we can knock up a garage in the next village to come and pull the car out.'

'Perhaps we'll come across a farm and be able to phone a garage,' Sara suggested hopefully.

'Perhaps. But with the kind of luck I've been having since I met you, I very much doubt it,' he replied, his mouth twisting wryly as he looked at the car.

Still subdued by the shock of the accident, Sara said

with difficulty, 'It was my fault. I distracted you. I'm sorry.'

He turned to look down at her again, his eyes glinting in the darkness. 'You do choose the darnedest times to pick a fight,' he agreed sardonically. Then briskly, 'Well, there's no point in standing here.' He bent to pick up the cases. 'You can carry the torch.'

They set off down the road, Sara holding the umbrella high after she had lifted it to a comfortable height for herself and Alex had complained that she was trying to poke his eyes out. For what seemed like miles they plodded on through the rain. Sara's arms ached from holding up the umbrella, the shoes that had seemed so comfortable when she had bought them a week ago now rubbed her feet in a dozen places and her wet trousers clung damply to her legs.

Alex stopped beside her and put the cases down. Gratefully Sara changed hands, holding the umbrella in the crook of her right arm while she rubbed her left to restore the circulation. She hardly heard Alex as he said, 'Look, isn't that a light?'

'Where?'

'Over to the right.'

She saw it then, the square of a lighted window several hundred yards away. 'I see it. But how do we get there?'

'There must be a track leading to it further along. Keep flashing the torch along that side of the road.'

Sara opened her mouth to inform him that she wasn't a complete moron, then shut it again, the incident with the car keeping her silent.

Soon they came to a break in the stone wall with a rough track leading from it. Fastened to a post was a crudely painted signboard with the words 'Hayscroft

Farm'. The farm track was furrowed with deep tractor
ruts full of muddy water. Carefully they picked their
way along the higher parts, but twice Sara slipped and
the water came over her shoes. Miserably she gritted
her teeth and plodded on. The light came from a small,
stone-built farmhouse surrounded by barns and out-
houses. A gate barred the way to a yard that was a sea
of mud. There was also a strong smell of pigs. Sara
gave a groan when the torch lit up the filthy state of
the yard.

'Stay here,' said Alex. 'I'll take the cases first and then
come back and carry you across.'

For a moment Sara was deliciously tempted to play
the frail female and do as he said, but better the mud
than Alex Brandon. 'I can manage, thanks,' she replied
firmly.

He shrugged. 'Suit yourself.' Pushing open the gate
he led the way across the yard. They were almost at the
door when he said, 'Did you shut the gate?'

Sara was concentrating on trying to hold her trousers
out of the mud as well as carry the torch and umbrella.
'What? No, I didn't.'

'Then go back and shut it.'

'What on earth for? No one's going anywhere on a
night like this.'

He turned exasperatedly. 'Don't you know the first
rule on a farm is to always shut the gates? We won't
endear ourselves to the farmer if his livestock get out
and go wandering over the hills.'

'The way those pigs smell we'd be doing him a
favour,' she retorted, but after a moment turned irritably back to shut the gate.

Alex didn't wait for her but went straight to the
farmhouse door and banged on it loudly. The man

who opened it peered out into the night at him.

'Good evening. I'm sorry to disturb you,' Alex began, 'but we've had to leave my car back down the road. I wonder if we might use your phone to call for help?'

The farmer, a scraggy, weatherbeaten man, looked at him for a moment longer, then saw Sara behind him. 'You've a lass with you? You'd best come in.'

Gratefully they went through the doorway which entered straight into a large kitchen-cum-living-room with an old-fashioned solid fuel range against one wall, its iron doors open to reveal a hot fire.

'Some people in trouble, Mary,' the farmer said to the woman who had risen to her feet from a fireside chair as they entered.

Sara took one look at the glowing coals and headed for them. The woman clucked with dismay at the sight of her clothes. 'You never walked along the track in yon? Ee, lass, you'll catch your death! Wait now while I make you a cup of hot, strong tea.'

'Thank you,' Sara said through chattering teeth as she held her hands out to the warmth.

'You are on the phone?' Alex was asking the farmer.

'Oh, aye. But it'll no do you any good to use it, for the garage in Hayscroft is closed for the night and won't be open until the morning.'

'Is there anywhere that would hire a car out to us, then?'

The man shook his head. 'There's only the garage.'

'It looks as if we'll have to put up somewhere for the night, then. I'd be very glad to pay you for your trouble if you could drive us to the nearest hotel yourself,' Alex added.

With a slow smile the farmer again shook his head. 'If I'd had a car available I would have offered it at once, but my Range Rover is itself in the garage to be serviced.'

Sara looked at Alex in dismay at the thought of having to go out again in the pouring rain and wade across the muddy yard and along the track.

He gave a slight nod and turned again to the farmer. 'I wonder, could we intrude on your hospitality even further and ask you if you could put us up for the night? A couple of chairs in front of the fire would do.'

'Bless you,' his wife said before he could answer, 'of course you can stay. I wouldn't turn a dog out on a night like this. And we can do better than a couple of chairs. You can have our spare room. I'll fill some hot water bottles and put them in the bed for you this minute. And then I'll cook you up a bite of supper.'

'Oh, but. . . .' Sara opened her mouth to explain that they weren't married, but Alex quickly interrupted her.

'That's extremely kind of you, Mrs . . .?'

'Mrs Hawkins. And my husband's name is Ted.'

'Thank you, Mrs Hawkins. We'd be very glad to accept your offer, wouldn't we, darling?' he added, turning towards Sara and frowning at her meaningly.

'Oh, yes. Yes, thank you,' she replied in rather a dazed voice.

'Good. I see you've got your cases with you, so why don't you change out of those wet clothes and I'll dry yours off in front of the stove?' Mrs Hawkins suggested to Sara. 'If you'll follow me I'll show you upstairs.'

Alex passed Sara her suitcase and looked at her mockingly when she shot him a malevolent glance before following her hostess up the narrow staircase.

The spare room was low and beamed, with an old-fashioned dresser with a fly-blown mirror against one wall and a large, high bed with a brass bedstead against the other. It was also extremely cold.

'There's a bathroom next door,' Mrs Hawkins told her with some pride. 'There's not many hill farms as has a bathroom. I'll leave you to change while I get the hot bottles.'

Stripping off her wet things, Sara put on a terry bathrobe and went into the bathroom looking forward to a hot soak. It wouldn't have been out of place in a museum! The only source of hot water was an archaic-looking geyser that she couldn't get to work no matter how she tried, while all the time she was getting colder and colder. In the end she had to settle for a cold wash down and scurried back to the bedroom to put on a thick sweater and a pair of jeans. The big bed looked very inviting and she realised suddenly how tired she was. It had been a long, worrying day and she yearned to curl up under the thick feather eiderdown. But *not*, she thought belligerently, with Alex beside her. If his hasty interruption when she had been going to tell their hosts they weren't married meant that he had ideas in that direction, then she was prepared to disillusion him—in no uncertain terms!

She brushed her hair, but when she went to put on fresh make-up gave a gasp of dismay as she realised that she had left her handbag in the car. Darn! Without make-up she felt strangely naked, and definitely at a disadvantage when it came to dealing with Alex Brandon. So it was with a rather defiant air about her that she went down to the living-room again, ready to snap at Alex if he so much as raised an eyebrow when he saw her.

The long table in the centre of the room was already laid for supper and Mrs Hawkins ushered her into a chair next to Alex. He and the farmer seemed to be in the middle of an engrossing conversation on the future of pig-farming in the Common Market. His eyes swept over her as she came in, taking in her figure-hugging jeans and resting for a moment on her clean face and the distinct challenge in her brown eyes. Without comment he turned away and resumed his conversation. Heaped plates of potato pie were placed in front of them and Sara tucked into hers hungrily, the hot food and the fire dispelling the cold inside her until at last she sat back, warm and replete and feeling terribly sleepy. She helped Mrs Hawkins to do the washing-up and then her hostess signified that it was time for bed. Evidently they kept early hours on the farm. Once in the bedroom, Sara hastily changed into her nightdress and was glad that she had brought a full, white cotton one with long sleeves and a delicately tucked and embroidered bodice. Turning out the light, she had to literally climb into the high bed and hastily dived between the covers before she could get cold again. The stone hot bottles had done their work well and the bed was warm and cosy.

Ten minutes later the door was pushed open and the light switched on again as Alex came into the room carrying his case and shut the door behind him. Sara had been prepared for this; she sat up in bed and looked at him angrily. 'Just what was the big idea of giving the impression we were married?'

He opened his case and put a few things on the top of the dresser. 'I didn't fancy spending the night on a chair,' he answered mildly.

'Well, that's a pity, because that's just where you're going to have to spend it. You can stay here until the Hawkins' are safely in bed and then go back down to the kitchen,' Sara told him determinedly, adding, 'Any ideas you've got about having a one-night stand with me you can put out of your mind here and now!'

'A one-night stand? What an extremely vulgar expression. I wonder where you learnt it.' He took off his shirt and threw it over the back of a chair, revealing a smooth chest and muscled arms. Then he came to sit on the edge of the bed while he took off his shoes. 'You should wait till you're asked. I have no designs on you —only the bed. I have no intention of spending an uncomfortable night propped up on a chair when we can both get a good night's sleep in that bed.' He rose and switched off the light and Sara heard him moving about in the darkness. Then the bed creaked as he began to climb into it.

'Don't you dare get in here!' Sara said angrily. She tried to reach out to push him away, but her hands encountered the bare skin of his shoulder. 'Where are your pyjamas?' she asked abruptly.

He chuckled in the darkness. 'Never wear the things.'

'What?' Sara shot out of the bed and hurried to turn on the light. Still standing by the door, she said furiously, 'Get out of that bed and go down to the kitchen!'

He raised an eyebrow. 'Like this?'

'No, you fool! You can get dressed again.'

Calmly Alex put his hands behind his head and looked at her sardonically. 'No way.'

'You louse! If you don't get out of here I'll scream!'

'Scream away—and get us both thrown out into the rain again.'

Sara glared at him resentfully, imagining the embarrassment of having the Hawkins' bursting in and trying to explain to them. 'If you were a gentleman you'd *offer* to sleep in the chair,' she told him viciously.

'And if you were a lady I might just do that. But you're a liberated twentieth-century career woman, remember? Equal rights and all that. Well, that's what I'm offering you: the equal right to half of this bed, and if that doesn't suit you then *you* go and sleep in the chair!'

'You pig! You know darn well I'll never share that bed with you.'

'Why not? I've already told you that masculine domineering women don't turn me on. You're quite safe from me. I prefer someone that acts and feels like a woman as well as looks like one. You can sleep on top of the covers if you're afraid,' he added.

'You're crazy. No man and woman ever shared a bed platonically.'

Alex's lip curled. 'You overrate yourself.' Then, 'Please yourself, I'm going to get some sleep.' He turned his back towards her and Sara wished she had a knife to stick in him. For a minute longer she stood by the door, undecided and getting very cold in her bare feet and thin nightdress. Then she snapped out the light; even if she had to stay awake all night she wouldn't share a bed with him. Groping her way to her clothes, she found her big coat and put it on over her nightdress, then curled up in a chair, her feet tucked under her for warmth. It would have been warmer in the kitchen, but she was afraid of waking the farmer and his wife if she tried to go down there in the darkness. And besides, she wasn't going to give Alex the satisfaction of having driven her out of the room. As the night wore on she began to get even colder, her teeth chattering, her hands and feet freezing, her limbs cramped. She toyed with getting dressed again, but the thought of taking off the coat and nightdress made her flesh cringe.

Eventually the noise of rain against the window panes stopped and later the moon came out to shine through the curtains. It outlined Alex's head against the whiteness of the pillows and she glared at him resentfully. Lord, how she hated him! She'd known him for scarcely more than a day, but already she felt more antagonistic towards him than anyone she had known in her whole life. He was hard and completely unfeeling. No wonder he wasn't married—no one in their right mind would ever put up with him. He stirred a little and the moon accentuated his high cheekbones, his thin, curved mouth and determined chin. Sara shivered again, not entirely from cold. He looked a hard man to cross, and he and she had crossed swords with a vengeance.

The eiderdown had slipped a little when he moved and hung over the edge of the bed. It gave her an idea. Slowly she pushed herself out of the chair as quietly as possible, but the old wood still creaked as she rose. Hardly daring to breathe lest she wake him, she crept towards the bed and gradually began to pull the eiderdown off. It slid, warm and bulky, into her arms. Turning gleefully, she went to tiptoe back to the chair and wrap herself in it.

'Put it back, Sara.' His voice made her jump.

'Why should I?' She snapped at him. 'You've got the bed and the blankets. The least you can do is to let me have the eiderdown.'

'All or nothing; the choice was yours. Now put it back.'

Sara tried to play on his sympathy. 'Alex, I'm freezing.'

'Serves you right,' he said unfeelingly.

'Oh!' she exploded. 'You're the most vile, rotten. . . . Oh, what's the use?' She flung the eiderdown back over the bed and went again to sit in the chair, colder than ever.

It was almost three in the morning before she gave in at last and came, shivering violently, to creep on top of the bed. As she inched her way further on, Alex's voice said softly, 'Little fool,' and he pulled the eiderdown over her, tucking her in, before going back to sleep.

Filtered sunlight shining through the floral patterned curtains woke Sara the next morning. She moved her head away and went to go back to sleep, but something dug into her and when she went to move she found that it was the buckle of her coat. She came awake with a jolt then, fully aware of her surroundings. Quickly she turned to look at the other side of the bed, then gave a gasp of relief when she saw it was empty, only the dent in the pillow showing where Alex's head had lain. Sitting up, she glanced at her watch and saw it was already eight o'clock, so she jumped quickly from the warmth of the bed and peered out into the narrow landing to see if the bathroom was free. The delicious scent of frying bacon and toast wafted up the stairs and made her hurry to wash and dress. She put on the jeans and sweater again, and crossing to the window, pulled the curtains back to look out. A thin film of mist lay over the grey hills as the warmth of the April sunshine dried the rain-soaked grass; sheep bleated to their little black-legged lambs in the lush green of the pastures and above them the sun-kissed sky was clear and cloudless. It looked so beautiful that Sara paused in brushing her hair to just stand and take it all in, to try and hold the picture in her memory forever.

But behind her she heard the door open and turned to see Alex standing in the doorway. Abruptly she walked towards the mirror and finished her hair, a slight flush on her face.

'Good morning,' he greeted her. 'I came to tell you that breakfast is ready.'

'Thanks, I'll be right down.'

But he didn't go away, instead leaning against the door jamb, his arms folded, calmly watching her. Today he was wearing a casual navy blazer over the polo sweater.

'Did you want something?' she asked pointedly, as she packed her nightdress in her case.

'No,' he replied equably. 'I just thought I'd wait for you.'

'Don't bother,' she replied tartly.

'Oh, it's no bother,' he assured her maddeningly. 'How old are you?' he asked after a moment.

'Twenty-six,' she answered automatically, then suspiciously, 'Why do you want to know?'

'Just curiosity. In those clothes and without make-up you don't look much older than Nicky.'

'I left my bag in the car,' she admitted, looking distastefully at her reflection in the spotted mirror.

'You should do it more often, it softens you. I thought you were a lot older—at least thirty.'

Sara threw her hairbrush into the case and slammed it shut. Without a word she stalked past him to go down the stairs.

'Tut, tut,' he murmured as she passed. 'Get out of the wrong side of the bed, Sara?'

Mrs. Hawkins greeted her with a friendly smile. 'Good morning, lassie. Did you sleep well?'

Sara's answering smile was rather stiff as she took a chair and Alex came to sit next to her, his arm along the back of her seat. 'Very well, thank you,' she replied, pulling the chair forward so that he had to move his arm.

Breakfast was a substantial meal and after it Ted Hawkins offered to get out his tractor and try to pull Alex's car out of the ditch. Sara stayed to chat to Mrs Hawkins for a while, but it was obvious that her hostess wanted to get on with her chores, so she borrowed a pair of wellingtons and wandered out to the back of the farm and across the field. The sun felt warm and pleasant on her face, the slight breeze bringing the scent of grass after rain. Sheep moved out of her way as she passed, but one black-faced lamb, top-heavy for its spindly legs, came running behind her, following her as she walked.

'Hey, I'm not your mother!' She turned round and laughingly picked it up. The creature bleated contentedly as she sat on a low stone wall and began to stroke it. The view from here was magnificent; the high, treeless hills with just enough cragginess in them to give a look of grandeur to the scene but not enough to make them forbidding. It was easy to see why people came here for holidays, she thought dreamily. But only for holidays; there was something about working in London, or any big city for that matter, that set the adrenalin going and gave a stimulus to life. Okay, so it was a rat race; thousands of people couldn't stand the pace and gratefully dropped out of it, but to those who could, those who weren't afraid to be ambitious, life could be heady and exciting. Exhausting too, when you worked for long periods under pressure, but always stimulating, always worthwhile.

Alex's voice calling her name broke into her thoughts and she turned to see him beckoning to her from the farm. She put down the lamb and shooed it away, but it persistently ran after her as she joined him, her blonde hair tousled by the breeze.

He grinned. 'You look like Mary and her little lamb.'

Sara laughed and smiled back, then looked quickly away; she had forgotten for a moment how much she disliked him. 'Did you get the car out?'

'Yes, it's waiting at the end of the track. I brought your bag for you. I thought you might want to put on your war-paint before we returned to civilisation,' he added mockingly.

Ignoring his remark, Sara hurried to get ready and collect her case. Mrs Hawkins lent her the boots again to walk down to the end of the track and came to see them off. Alex pressed some money into her hands to pay for their night's lodgings, and then they were waving the friendly couple goodbye as they set off again.

'And no more trying to pick up the trail. This time we're going straight to the Lake District,' Alex insisted grimly.

# CHAPTER FOUR

IT was early afternoon before they arrived at their destination, having stopped for lunch just after turning off the motorway. Sara directed Alex along the winding narrow lane towards Appleberry, Veronica Quinlan's house. She got out to open the five-barred wooden gate while Alex drove through, and looked at the house with something less than anticipation. It stood, square and grey among its screening trees, still leafless and only just beginning to bud after the long winter. The aged grey slate of the thick walls gave the house warmth and made it look friendly and inviting, but it was with some trepidation that Sara walked up to the door and rang the bell.

It was opened by a short, thinly energetic woman who greeted her with a warm smile and at her enquiring look answered, 'Aye, they're here. Came about an hour ago. I've got them both in the kitchen, eating as if they hadn't had anything for a month. You didn't tell me it was a boy-friend she was bringing,' Mrs Ogden added sharply.

'No, I didn't want Miss Quinlan worried unnecessarily,' Sara told her. 'This is Mr Alexander Brandon,' she added as Alex came to join her. 'He's the young man's uncle. Does Nicky's godmother know they're here yet?'

'Aye, I told her as soon as they arrived. She's getting up now and coming down. But she has to take it easy and not get too excited, you know that, Miss Sara.'

'Yes, I know.' She bit the tip of her finger, wondering what was best to do. Veronica Quinlan was still recovering from a major operation and her first care was that she shouldn't be upset in any way.

'Perhaps it would be best if you talked to Miss Quinlan first,' Alex suggested.

'Yes, I suppose so.' Sara looked at him suspiciously. 'What are you going to do?'

He gave a slightly crooked smile. 'I could do with some exercise. I'll take a walk and come back in half an hour. Does that give you enough time?' he asked with a trace of sarcasm.

Sara flushed. 'Yes, I think so,' she replied stiffly.

He turned on his heel and went back through the door, striding briskly down the gravel driveway.

Mrs Ogden looked at Sara consideringly. 'That's a well set-up young man. Is he married?'

Sara glared after him. 'No. No one but a fool would take him on.'

'Hm,' was the housekeeper's only comment, which could have meant anything. 'You'd better come up straightaway,' she advised, and led the way up the staircase with its rather worn carpet to a room on the right of the landing.

Knocking softly, Sara received an answering, 'Come in,' and entered the room to find Veronica Quinlan seated in front of the dressing-table slowly combing her smooth grey hair.

She smiled when she saw Sara, the lines of pain around her eyes disappearing momentarily. 'My dear child, how very nice to see you! But in rather unhappy circumstances, I'm afraid.' That was one thing Sara liked about Nicky's godmother, she always came straight to the point.

'Yes, and Nicky had no right to bring her troubles to you when you've been so ill. Shall I do your hair for you?' she offered.

'Thank you, dear, would you? I'm afraid I still find it hard to get my arm up quite that high, but I do better every day,' she added optimistically.

'Good for you.' Sara took the comb and began to arrange the older woman's hair while she told her all about Nicky's runaway romance. 'It's quite impossible, of course,' she finished. 'They're far too young to know their own minds, besides not being able to afford it.'

'But Nicky will have her father's money, won't she?'

'Not if I withhold it,' Sara said grimly. 'And I certainly don't intend to let her have it at her age. She and this boy would spend the lot in six months.'

'I always thought Nicky's father was extremely unwise when he made that will,' Veronica remarked as she selected a pair of earrings. 'One young girl in charge of another's destiny—it was bound to lead to trouble.'

Sara stiffened. 'Are you accusing me of not letting Nicky have the money out of jealousy?'

'Good heavens, no! I'm sure you're doing what you think is right,' she was assured. 'But I think Nicky would have been able to take it better from an older person, not felt driven to run away as she has.'

'You think Nicky's father should have asked you to be her guardian? I wish he had,' Sara said vehemently. 'Looking after her has been a constant worry. But you used to go abroad such a lot when you worked for that archaeologist that I suppose he didn't think it fair to ask you, whereas I was on hand in London.'

'Yes, dear, I know. Please don't think I'm criticising you.'

'Anyway, the fact still remains that Nicky's far too

young to even think about marriage.'

'I suppose so, although,' Veronica hesitated, 'I remember when I was seventeen I fell head over heels in love myself.'

'Did you?' Sara asked curiously. 'What happened? Did you grow out of it?'

'My parents thought I was far too young as well and said we had to wait. Naturally I obeyed them; one did obey one's parents in those days,' she smiled. 'But then the war came along and he went off to fight, he wasn't too young for that. I can still see him now in his uniform, waving to me from the train after I'd promised to wait for him.' She paused, a faraway look in her alert eyes, then her glance met Sara's in the mirror and she added flatly, 'But he didn't come back. He was killed at Dunkirk. And there was never anyone else, Sara, not in all these long years.' She stood up. 'And now let's go down and meet these runaways, shall we, and also this man you've brought with you?'

Taking her arm, Sara helped her down the stairs and into the drawing-room, settling her into a comfortable chair. The door bell rang again and she went to answer it. It was Alex. She introduced him to Veronica Quinlan and then he said, 'Let's get it over with, shall we?'

'All right, I'll get them.' Sara went to go to the kitchen, but there was no need; as she stepped into the hallway Nicky and a tall, lanky youth were coming towards her, shepherded by Mrs Ogden.

Nicky stopped dead when she saw Sara, a look of horrified dismay on her face. 'Oh, no!' She turned and clung to the boy. 'It's Sara, my horrible stepsister!'

Her face tightening angrily, Sara took a hasty step forward, but then a hand took hold of her elbow in a vice-like grip and Alex's voice, light and amused, said close behind her, 'And Richard's wicked uncle too. So now that we have all the characters why don't you come and say hallo to the fairy godmother?'

He propelled all of them back into the drawing-room and Sara noticed that Richard gave Alex an uneasy grin in answer to his own smile. Putting a hand on his nephew's shoulder, Alex stood beside him while Nicky threw herself on her knees beside her godmother's chair and looked tearfully up at her. Veronica took her hand and stroked her hair gently. 'It's all right, my child, don't worry. You can stay here as long as you like. This is your home, you know that.'

Sara's mouth twisted at the look of love and gratitude that came over Nicky's features. All very well, she thought rather resentfully, but that isn't going to help any.

His hand still on Richard's shoulder, Alex drew him forward to introduce him. 'This is my nephew, Richard French, Miss Quinlan. His parents live abroad, so I stand *in loco parentis* to him at the moment.'

The boy shook hands, a warm smile lighting up his thin face, and for a moment he reminded her vividly of Alex. Apart from this brief glimpse, there was, however, very little else that proclaimed their relationship; whereas Alex was broad and muscular with athletic hips, Richard was still an adolescent and looked as if he didn't get enough exercise. The studious type, Sara thought as she sized him up dispassionately. Alex glanced up and saw her watching Richard. Immediately he moved nearer to him, as if shielding him from her. Sara looked at him sardonically for a moment and then turned away to cross to a chair and listen while Nicky poured her version of the story into Veronica's ears.

'Yes, dear, I quite understand how you feel,' her god-mother assured her when she had finished. 'But you know, there's nothing I can do. Your father left you in Sara's charge, not mine.' At this Nicky looked at Sara with antagonism hardly short of hate in her eyes. It hurt, but Sara was able to return the look impassively. 'But what I do suggest,' Veronica went on, 'is that you all stay here for a few days so that Sara can get to know Richard better. You did rather spring your news on everyone, you know. Naturally Sara wasn't going to let you marry someone she hadn't even met.' She turned to smile at Alex. 'And Mr Brandon must stay too, if he can spare the time.'

'I should be delighted. Thank you,' Alex returned with a smile.

If *he* can spare the time, Sara thought indignantly. No one bothers to wonder if I can!

Mrs Ogden came in then with a coffee tray and Sara was kept busy pouring it and handing out cakes and biscuits while Alex talked to Richard over by the win-dow and Nicky held an almost whispered conversation with Veronica, which was evidently about Sara because Nicky deliberately didn't look at her except to sneak sidelong glances to see if she was listening.

Sara sipped her coffee, her resentment growing, un-til she put down her cup and stood up abruptly. 'If everyone's staying Mrs Ogden will want help prepar-ing the rooms, so if you'll excuse me, Veronica, I'll go and help her.'

'Oh, please don't rush away,' Veronica replied. 'We've hardly begun to talk.'

'On the contrary, you all seem to be doing very well without me,' Sara returned tartly before she stepped briskly from the room.

She found Mrs Ogden making up the bed in one of

the smaller back rooms. 'I thought I'd put the young man in here,' she told her. 'And you and Miss Nicky can share the big room next to Miss Quinlan's.'

And that should make for a jolly few days, Sara thought resignedly. No escape from Nicky's sulking even at night. She turned her attention to the task in hand with her characteristic energy and afterwards went to the kitchen with Mrs Ogden to help prepare dinner.

'Have you got enough food in? Four more people dumped on you suddenly are going to make a lot of work, I'm afraid.'

'Don't you worry none, Miss Sara. I can cope. And there's plenty of food in the freezer, but I shall have to go and get some fresh vegetables tomorrow.'

'I can do that for you,' Sara offered. 'I'll walk into Lowmere in the morning. Perhaps I can persuade Nicky to come along so that we can have a talk.'

Dinner began as a rather strained meal but gradually relaxed as Alex and Veronica Quinlan deliberately drew everyone into the conversation. Soon Richard was chatting away about his college and his career prospects and Nicky—who was sitting as far away from Sara as possible—was making her godmother laugh with the story of a play she had been in at school.

'The last rehearsal was hilarious. I only hope the play goes off all right on the night.'

'Well, you'll be able to find out when you go back, won't you?' Sara remarked deliberately.

There was a sudden silence. Nicky bit her lip and bent to her plate. Richard looked at her for a moment and then turned away, but Alex stared at her across the table with something like contempt in his eyes before Veronica changed the subject.

Sara squared her shoulders, uncaring. Let them think

what they liked; everyone had been behaving as if Nicky was going to get her own way. It was about time she was reminded that she was still a schoolgirl and in her charge.

After dinner she said pointedly to Nicky, 'As we're all here on your account I think the least you can do is to offer to help with the washing-up.'

Nicky turned bright red. 'I was going to,' she said sullenly, adding defiantly, 'It'll be good practice for when I get married.'

Richard stood up saying, 'I'll come and help too,' and followed her from the room.

'Good lord, that's the first time I've ever heard him offer to do any domestic chores,' Alex remarked. 'Love must be having a mellowing influence on him.'

'Don't worry, I expect he'll soon grow out of it and become a trainee male chauvinist again,' Sara said sweetly.

Alex looked as if he was about to make a biting retort, but remembered Veronica's presence and instead turned to her to ask her about her travels abroad. He couldn't have asked a better question as far as Veronica was concerned, and she was soon telling him all about the digs she had accompanied in the role of research secretary to a famous archaeologist who had died a few years ago. Showing him a glass cabinet containing various shards and relics, she talked animatedly for nearly an hour, with Alex asking the occasional question which showed that he had some knowledge of the subject.

Sara was content to just sit and sip a sherry while she watched them, having seen and heard it all before. Alex was very good with and for Veronica, she realised, leading her on to tell him anecdotes, making her laugh, and

quite simply setting out to use all his masculine wiles
to charm her. And charm her he did; she was looking
far better and younger than she had before dinner. It
was then that Sara realised just what a devastating
effect Alex could have on a woman—any woman. With
his dark good looks, physical strength, and that power
he had of making a woman feel she was the one person
in the world he wanted to be with, he must have left a
trail of disappointed women behind him. So why hadn't
he ever married? Sara pondered the question as she
watched him examining a piece of Etruscan pottery. He
probably hasn't found anyone he considers good
enough for him, she thought cynically, or else he
spreads the charm among too many women and they
see through him. But she didn't really believe it was the
latter, it was only she, on whom he hadn't turned any
charm at all, who could observe him that dispassionately. He's probably got a dolly bird tucked away in a
flat somewhere and doesn't feel the need to get married
when he can get what he wants without it, she decided
disparagingly.

As if guessing her thoughts, Alex glanced up then
and caught her studying him. His left eyebrow rose sardonically and Sara felt herself start to flush guiltily.
Quickly she rose. 'Veronica, don't you think it's time
you went upstairs? You must be tired.'

'Good heavens, is that the time? You're quite right,
Sara, I shall feel fagged in the morning.' She turned to
Alex. 'Goodnight, Mr Brandon. I hope you haven't
been too bored with my chatter.'

"On the contrary,' Alex took her hand, 'I've seldom
enjoyed an evening more. You must tell me about the
other pieces another time. And my name is Alex,' he
reminded her.

Sara helped the older woman upstairs and to prepare for bed before Mrs Ogden came up with a nightcap. The housekeeper seemed to have an uncanny knowledge of when she was needed—that, or just good ears, Sara thought as she went downstairs again. She looked in the kitchen, but it was empty, the crockery all neatly stacked in the cupboard.

'Do you know where Nicky and Richard are?' she asked as she went back into the drawing-room.

'They went for a walk.' Alex rose as she came in. 'Do you want another drink?'

'No. Why didn't you stop them? This would have been a good opportunity to get this thing settled once and for all.'

He poured himself a whisky from the decanter on the sideboard and then went to sit in the armchair by the fire, his long legs stretched out in front of him. 'Because I think it would be better to do as Veronica suggested and let you get to know Richard first, He's quite a nice kid, you know.'

'Well, I'm hardly likely to get to know him when he's out necking with Nicky, am I?'

'Didn't you neck when you were a teenager?' he asked casually.

'That has nothing to do with it.'

'Hasn't it? I rather think it has.' He looked at her keenly. 'From the beginning of this affair you've been against it out of all proportion, not bothering to try to see Nicky's side or even asking to meet Richard. You're holding your power over her like some old-fashioned autocrat and seem to enjoy making her miserable. At first I thought it was because you were more interested in your job, but it's not entirely that. So what is it, Sara? Why are you being so dogmatic?'

'I'm nothing of the sort. I just want what's best for Nicky,' Sara retorted.

'Do you? Or is it,' his eyes sharpened, 'or is it that you're jealous?'

'Jealous?' Sara rose indignantly. 'Of Richard? You must be crazy!'

Alex, too, got to his feet and came to stand beside her. 'Not of Richard—of marriage. Or of just being loved,' he added, watching her closely.

Sara stared at him speechlessly for a moment. 'How dare you suggest that!' she said angrily at last. 'You're out of your tiny mind! Why don't you stick to your computers? Mindless machines are obviously more in your line than human beings.'

'Possibly. But in this case I'm pretty sure I'm right. Oh, no, you're not running out on this one,' he added, catching her arm as she went to walk away. 'You've got a chip on your shoulder as big as a plank, and I intend to find out why.'

'Let go of me!' Sara said furiously. 'My private life is nothing to do with you.'

'It is when it affects Nicky, and therefore Richard. I'm not having his life messed up by a frustrated female.'

'Of all the nerve! I am *not* frustrated. And I thought we agreed that marriage to Nicky would ruin Richard's life.'

'I'm beginning to have second thoughts about that. It might be just what he needs. But don't try to change the subject. We're talking about you, not Richard.'

'You're doing all the talking, you mean. And drawing your own stupid conclusions,' she retorted.

'And what were you doing when you were watching me earlier on? From the look on your face you'd summed me up as something not much better than a gigolo.'

'I can hardly help it, can I, when that's the impression you give?' Sara returned nastily.

Alex's jaw tensed and his grip on her arm tightened until she winced. He smiled unpleasantly. 'You don't like it when I use force on you, do you? Never mind, you can always take up judo, then no one will be able to master you.' His dark eyes glinted down at her. 'What happened, Sara? Did the man you wanted get away? God, I pity the poor devil. He must have been through hell before he found the courage to walk out on you. Especially if he cared about you.'

Numbly Sara stared at him, unable to speak.

'And now you've built so thick a wall around yourself that you resent any man you can't put down—and any woman who's got what you lost,' he added forcefully.

Sara felt her nails digging into her hands as she strove to control herself. 'How dare you speak to me like that?' she demanded with hatred in her eyes. 'What right have you got to probe into my past? I bet you've walked out on dozens of women. For your information, I could have married several times if that was all I'd wanted, but I couldn't because I....' She stopped, shaking with anger, her hands clenched into fists.

'Why not, Sara? Why couldn't you marry?' Alex put his other hand on her right arm to emphasise his question.

For a moment she stared at him, an aching tightness in her throat, then she put up her arms and shook him off. 'Oh, go to hell!' And she ran from the room and up the stairs.

Once in the room she was to share with Nicky, Sara sat on the edge of her bed, her head in her hands.

Gradually her pounding heart slowed and she was able to lie back on her bed in a shaft of moonlight from the window. She hadn't bothered to switch on the lamps and the moonlit objects in the unfamiliar room had an almost luminous quality. Deliberately she forced her mind to concentrate on the row with Alex. Why had she got so upset? Why did she always lose control whenever she argued with him? But that last was an easy one to answer; whether he was being at his most charming or scathingly contemptuous, he was a man with whom it was impossible to be indifferent.

She tried to think rationally, trying to analyse what had happened. His accusations had, of course, brought back all too vividly that first love affair. Had its failure made her bitter? She had never thought so before; had regarded it only as a salutary lesson not to fall for the first person who came along. Perhaps in some ways it had served to convince her that Nicky's romance couldn't possibly be the real thing, but as for using her power over Nicky to make her miserable! The man was mad, completely mad. So why had it hurt so much? Sara sighed and turned over. Could it be that Alex Brandon in turn enjoyed the power he seemed to have over her, the power to goad her into losing her temper? Or perhaps he was just piqued because she hadn't fallen for him, she thought cynically, and if he couldn't rouse her emotions one way then he'd rouse them the other.

Well, there was one simple solution to that problem. She got up and started to undress, the moonlight silvering the soft curves of her body. She would just have to make darn sure in future that she didn't let him get under her skin. Complete indifference was the only weapon she had against Alex Brandon and she intended to use it, however hard he tried to pierce it. In fact, build the wall around herself that he claimed she already had. And Nicky? Sara climbed rather wearily into bed. Tomorrow she would insist on getting Nicky alone and finally having that talk with her.

Surprisingly she fell asleep straight away, not even hearing Nicky when she crept into the room later, and in the morning she awoke feeling refreshed and ready to face the day. Nicky was still asleep and from past experience Sara knew that she wouldn't stir until forcibly shaken, so she felt no compunction in opening the curtains and pushing the window wide to let in the spring sunshine. She leant out, savouring the view down through the garden to the lake set among the ring of fells. The garden was thickly planted with Lent lilies, the same type of daffodil that Wordsworth wrote about at his cottage at nearby Grasmere. The scent from them rose to meet her on the morning air and she closed her eyes to take in the heady perfume.

'Good morning.' The voice below her roused her from her reverie and she looked down to see Alex standing in the garden, watching her.

Now how do you greet a man you had a blazing row with only the night before? she wondered. For a moment she thought of ignoring him completely, but it seemed pretty pointless and would only create more tension in an already taut atmosphere. Then she remembered her resolve not to let him get under her skin, so instead she gave him a dazzling smile and answered, 'Good morning. Do you always get up this early?'

His eyebrows rose slightly at the smile. 'Why don't you come down and join me?'

'Why not?' Sara turned back into the room and after taking a quick bath dressed in a cream silk shirt and a pair of brown cord trousers with a matching loose-knit sweater to wear over the shirt. She applied her make-up—her warpaint as Alex had so charmingly called it—very carefully. Somehow she had the feeling that it was going to be a long, hard day and she was going to need all the confidence she could muster to fight Alex.

He was waiting for her in the kitchen, sitting at the table drinking coffee and talking to Mrs Ogden.

It was the housekeeper who greeted her first. 'Morning, Miss Sara. Would you like your breakfast now or when the others get up?'

'Just coffee for now, thanks. Don't get up, I'll get it.' She poured herself a cup and leaned back against the sink while she drank it, and listened to Alex drawing Mrs Ogden out to tell him about the years she had spent in her native Lancashire where she had run a guest house in Morecambe.

'But then my Alf died and there didn't seem to be any point in carrying on somehow. Then I saw Miss Quinlan's advert and I've been here ever since. Nearly fifteen years now, it is.'

She chattered on happily and Sara realised unbelievingly that even the indomitable Mrs Ogden was falling under Alex's spell. But presently he rose and came over to her.

'Coming for a stroll round the garden?' he invited.

Putting down her cup, she replied casually, 'If you like.'

By mutual accord they made their way down the stone path towards the lake. The remains of a large, once imposing boathouse stood at the water's edge, but now the roof had partly collapsed and the timbers were damp and rotten.

'What lake is this?' he asked.

'Lowmere. It's one of the smallest, but I think one of the prettiest.'

He nodded towards the ruins of the boathouse. 'It's a shame that that's been let go, but I don't suppose Veronica is very keen on boating.'

'She used to be before she was ill. She wouldn't have let it get in such a state if she could have afforded to look after it, but unfortunately inflation caught up with her investments and I suppose the house had to come first.'

'It wouldn't take a lot to repair it,' Alex remarked as he examined the building more closely.

'There used to be a boat somewhere along the bank. Yes, here it is.' Sara pushed aside some screening bushes and showed him a tarpaulin-covered rowing boat upside down on the bank. 'When we came up here for holidays we used to row across the lake to that island over there.'

'Is it still seaworthy? Let's have a look.' Alex pulled off the tarpaulin and almost before she knew it Sara was helping to lower the boat into the water. 'It seems sound enough, and the oars are here too.' He put the oars in the boat and then got in himself. 'Come on, let's try it out.'

She hesitated. 'Now?'

'It will give you an appetite for breakfast. You needn't be afraid,' he added drily when she still demurred, 'I don't intend to give you a ducking.'

For a moment Sara glared at him, then shrugged, 'All right.'

He rowed the old boat easily and well, sending it scudding over the water towards the island she had mentioned. It made her remember other times when

they had taken the boat out when she was still at school
and Nicky just a small child. It had been fun then, all
of them together on the few times that her stepfather
had been able to get away from his business. She remembered how worried her mother had always been
that Nicky might fall overboard. But then she had always been protective towards the younger girl and very
close to her husband, so that Sara had often felt shut
out, an outsider. They had been kind, of course, but she
had felt as if she didn't completely belong and had
sometimes resented the love that had once been all her
own being transferred to this new family.

She trailed her hands in the water, a dark, hurt look
in her eyes. They came to the island, but when Alex
asked her if she wanted to land there she shook her
head.

'No, we'd better be getting back so that I can help
Mrs Ogden with the breakfasts.'

'I ought to make you row going back,' he told her
mockingly. 'Just so that we stay equal, of course.'

'It was your idea, so you can row,' she retorted, refusing to be drawn.

Halfway back he paused to rest, the water lapping
gently against the boat. It was very quiet, you could
hardly even hear the birds as they flew busily among
their nests in the trees that grew right down to the
water's edge. A heron, its grey wings translucent in the
sunlight, glided out from the island to swoop suddenly
towards the lake and emerge with a fish in its beak.

'Does it get very busy here in the summer?' Alex
asked.

'Pretty busy, but nowhere near as much as the larger
lakes. This one isn't really big enough for yachts and

power boats, so you mostly only get canoeists and campers.'

'I gather from Veronica that Nicky spends most summer holidays here.'

'Yes, she always has since our parents died.'

'You don't see much of her, then?'

Sara looked at him defensively. 'I see as much of her as I can. She always stays with me at half-term and Christmas, and I take my holidays to coincide with hers. Unfortunately there are few firms that are willing to give you three months' holiday a year, which is what Nicky gets,' she added bitingly.

'Couldn't she have stayed in your flat while you were at work?'

'A young girl on her own all day in London? She'd either have become bored to death or have got into the wrong company. It was better for her to come here.'

'I see.' His eyes ran over her. 'I thought it might have been for another reason.'

There was an inflection in his voice that suddenly made Sara become very still. 'What reason?' she asked slowly.

'I thought you might have had a man living with you and didn't want Nicky around.'

Sara's fingers dug deeply into the side of the boat, her knuckles as white as her face. Her first instinct was to let fly at him furiously, but then she remembered her resolve to be patient. Summoning up all her willpower, she forced herself to relax and look at him under her lashes. 'Which man do you mean?' she asked sweetly.

Alex drew in his breath sharply and looked at her searchingly. 'How many have you had?'

'Oh, I lost count after the first dozen,' she told him airily.

A grudging look of admiration came into his eyes as he picked up the oars and started to row again. 'All right, Sara, I give you victory on that one. But if you won't tell me then I shall just have to draw my own conclusions, won't I?'

'Well, that shouldn't be hard; you've been doing it ever since you met me,' she parried.

'No more than you have—and I'm willing to bet that mine are more accurate than yours.'

He pulled into the bank then and Sara was careful not to make any comments; her new resolve was already stretched very thin and only by keeping her mouth firmly shut could she hope to retain it. So they walked back to the house in silence and Sara was relieved to see that Nicky and Richard were already up.

'Breakfast's ready,' Mrs Ogden told them as they came in. 'Come and sit down before it gets cold.'

'I'm sorry, I should have stayed and helped you,' Sara apologised.

'No need, Miss Nicky helped instead.'

When breakfast was over Sara turned to her sister. 'Mrs Ogden needs some fresh vegetables, so I thought we might walk into Lowmere to get them for her.'

Nicky opened her mouth to refuse, but Alex cut in, 'Good idea. Richard can come with me into Keswick; I want to get the car checked over and I need a new reflector on the back. The other one got smashed recently.'

Sara flushed, remembering just how the car had got damaged.

'Why can't we all go to Keswick?' Nicky asked truculently.

Alex leaned forward and put a finger under her chin to tilt her head. 'Because, young lady, Richard and I

want to have a talk—man to man. So do as you're told
and go with Sara.'

'Oh! All right.' And Nicky ran willingly off to get her
coat, leaving Sara staring after her; she had been fully
prepared to face a long argument, but Alex had accom-
plished it in two seconds. She turned and found him
looking at her mockingly, his eyes glinting with amusement. The message in them was plain enough to read
and made Sara glare back at him before she went to
get the shopping list from Mrs Ogden.

The two sisters strolled down the lane that lay
parallel to the lake and in the beauty of the morning
even Nicky couldn't stay sullen for long. Sara still
found it difficult to broach the subject, but it had to be
done. She squared her shoulders determinedly and said
as casually as she could, 'Richard seems a nice boy.'

Nicky turned a surprised face to her. 'Oh, he is. He's
wonderful. Do you really like him, Sara?'

'As I said, he seems nice enough. But still a boy,
Nicky.'

'Well, he'll get older,' her sister pointed out with
simple logic.

Sara smiled slightly. 'That's true. But he's hardly in a
position to support a wife, especially one who has no
training for any kind of a career.'

'It is possible to train and be married, you know.'

'Yes, but not for anything worthwhile if you haven't
got any A levels. And don't look at me like that, Nicky;
I haven't said that you can't marry him ever, only that
you can't marry him *now*. If you go to university and
get a degree life will have a far better quality for you
both. You'll be able to. . . .'

'Oh, don't give me that lecture again, Sara! I've
heard it too often. I *knew* that was why you wanted to

get me by myself. And I suppose Richard is getting the same lecture from his uncle.'

'Yes, because we both want the best for you.' Sara stopped and pulled her sister to a halt beside her. 'Nicky, please try to look at this with your head, without your emotions getting in the way. Can't you see that although this is wonderful now, that feeling might not last? In two or three years you'll have changed and so will Richard, you'll be two entirely different people. And if you've grown apart then there'll be terrible unhappiness for both of you. And what if you get pregnant, have you thought of that?'

Nicky's face suddenly went bright red and she turned her head away and began to walk on again.

'You've seen girls at school who come from split families, do you dare to take the risk of inflicting that sort of life on a child?'

Sara pressed home the point as hard as she could, but Nicky suddenly turned round to face her. 'Yes, I dare,' she answered vehemently. 'Because I love Richard and he loves me. All right, so we're young. But we'll be together and we'll face things together. And as soon as Richard gets his degree and gets a job he'll support me. Until then we'll have Father's money to live on.'

'Oh, no, you won't!' Sara said angrily. 'Your father wanted you to have the best education you could. He wanted you to have all the things that I . . .' she covered the slip hurriedly, 'that he never had. And using it to support someone else just isn't on. Answer me this, Nicky: do you think your father would have let you marry at your age if he'd still been alive?'

The younger girl stared at her white-faced for a long moment and then tears began to fall down her cheeks. 'Why did you have to say that? You're cruel, Sara.' She put up a shaking hand to wipe away the tears. 'No, I don't suppose he would have wanted me to. But at least he'd have tried to understand, wouldn't have been cold and unfeeling like you. But you can't stop me marrying him, Sara. I'll be eighteen in September and then I'll be able to marry Richard whether you like it or not!'

'Yes, you will,' Sara answered quietly. 'But you'll have married without my blessing, so you won't get any money until you're twenty-five. Why don't you put *that* to Richard and see how he likes it?'

'It won't make any difference. I keep trying to tell you that we love each other, but you won't listen! Well, you can withhold the money, spend it on yourself for all I care. We'll manage without it!' And Nicky turned defiantly and strode on ahead.

Sara looked after her distressfully before following more slowly. She should have known that Nicky would never listen to reason in this mood. She had always been given anything that she wanted, and Richard had just taken the place of a new doll or a bicycle. She wanted him and she intended to have him.

Their shopping in the little village of grey stone houses was done in a strained silence, but on the way back Sara broached the second topic that she had wanted to discuss. 'Why did you come here to Veronica's house, Nicky? You know how ill she's been.'

'Well, I didn't know you were going to follow me here, did I? And I had nowhere else to go.'

'She mustn't be upset by all this,' Sara warned. 'It would be best if we all left as soon as possible.'

'Veronica's said that I can stay as long as I like. Richard and I wouldn't have been any trouble. It's *you* who's doing all the arguing and upsetting everyone,'

Nicky pointed out hostilely. 'So why don't *you* go away and leave us alone?'

'It's about time,' Sara returned bitingly, 'that you grew up and learned that you can't have everything your own way. You're thoroughly spoilt and selfish. Why don't you admit that you didn't give Veronica's condition a thought before you came hareing up here like some heroine in a Victorian melodrama? You knew darn well that I'd guess where you were going and follow you. You just wanted to get Veronica on your side and couldn't care less what it did to her health?'

'That isn't true. I came here because I needed her,' Nicky shouted. 'It's you who's making her excited, you who's being mean and horrible, you who won't....'

But that was as far as she got, because Sara slapped her on the cheek. 'Stop it! You're getting hysterical.' She tried to hold the younger girl to her, but Nicky gave her one look of pure hatred and thrust her away. Then she dropped the bag of groceries she was carrying and ran to climb over a fence and run away across the fields.

Sara called after her, but she knew it was futile. Resignedly she stooped to pick up the potatoes that had fallen from the bag and continued on the way back to the house, the heavy bags weighing her down so that she couldn't hurry. When she finally got back to Appleberry, Mrs Ogden told her that Alex had phoned to say that the car would take longer than he anticipated and he wouldn't be back until later in the afternoon.

'And Miss Nicky came in and rushed up to your bedroom and locked the door,' the housekeeper added in dire tones.

'Oh, great, now I won't be able to change until she

comes out. And knowing Nicky she's quite likely to stay there all day.'

'She'll come out fast enough when her young man gets back, don't you fret. Why don't you take the tray upstairs and have lunch with Miss Quinlan? She's tired today and she'll like a bit of company.'

Sara carried up the loaded tray and found Veronica sitting up in bed resting against the pillows. She smiled as Sara entered and helped her to unload the tray on to the bed table.

'It's good of you to keep me company. I gather you gave Nicky a good talking to?'

Shrugging her shoulders, Sara said ruefully, 'I tried, but it didn't do any good. She's being thoroughly obstinate and seems to resent me completely.' She paused unhappily. 'She even seemed to hate me.'

'Oh, she'll get over it,' Veronica said comfortably. 'She's only jealous.'

'Jealous? Why on earth should she be?'

Veronica's eyebrows rose. 'I should have thought that was obvious. You're beautiful and she's almost plain. You have a perfect figure and she's dumpy. She knows that you only have to crook your finger and dishy men like Alex Brandon will flock round you. You have drive and ambition and you're a success. Need I say more?'

Sara was looking at her in some amusement. 'Yes, you can tell me where you learned to describe men as dishy?'

Veronica's eyes twinkled. 'From Nicky, of course. She was mad about some French pop star last year and that was her latest word. And you must admit that Alex is dishy,' she added.

'I suppose so, if you like that terribly suave type.'

'But you don't?' Veronica asked her interestedly.

'Lord, no, he's not my type at all. Too clever and knowledgeable about women by half,' Sara said firmly. Then, reverting to their earlier subject, 'But it isn't true, you know, Veronica. Nicky isn't jealous of me. She told me that she doesn't want my kind of life. She just wants to settle down and get married.'

'Possibly because she knows in her heart that that's the only kind of life she could make a success of. She isn't very clever and she isn't beautiful. She could never even begin to compete with you in a career, but with a marriage she'll have beaten you already.'

Sara stared. 'Are you trying to tell me that Nicky wants to get married just to spite me?'

Veronica laughed. 'Good heavens, no! But I think she could very well feel that she's found someone she could love and who would be content with her, someone she's afraid she might never find again. And you're the one who's standing in her way. Think about it,' she added, and then changed the subject.

And Sara did think about it, long and hard. She phoned up the local garage and arranged to hire a car for the rest of the day, then she drove herself deep into the heart of the countryside and parked high up on the Kirkstone Pass road where she could sit and look at the stark beauty of the view. It had never occurred to her that Nicky might resent her success in business, or the way she looked, come to that. She sat and brooded about it for a long time and inevitably her thoughts also dwelt on the accusations that Alex had made. She felt bewildered and confused. But what was the point of all this soul-searching? The fact still remained that Nicky was too young. And if she wanted to marry out of jealousy then it was all the more reason to stop her, surely?

That point she settled in her mind, but then came the harder question: was she bitter about Nicky having inherited so much money, as Alex had accused her? Did she want to make Nicky fight for things just because she had had to fight for them too? Numbly she gazed out of the window, eyes unseeing. She twisted the idea round in her mind, seeing it first one way then the other. But she still hadn't come to any conclusion when she started the car again and drove down the twisty road into Ambleside to stop at a restaurant for a meal. It was busier here, the town thronged with early holidaymakers who gathered outside the souvenir and craft shops, their windows crammed with ornaments in green granite and packets of Kendal mint cakes, or took photographs of the tiny stone house built on a bridge that spanned the beck that ran through the town.

She took her time over the meal, deliberately not hurrying so that Nicky would have a chance to have a long talk with Veronica. It was obvious that anything that Sara tried to do would only exacerbate the situation and she fervently hoped that the older woman would be able to have a calming influence and perhaps make Nicky see a little sense. So after dinner she window-shopped for a time and then went into a hotel to while away an hour by having a drink in the bar. Being a woman alone brought its usual range of looks; speculative ones from the men who wondered if she was on the game, and resentful or pitying ones from the women.

Picking up a magazine, she flicked idly through the pages until she was interrupted by a well-built, middle-aged man. He addressed her with a knowing smile. 'Hallo there. All alone? Let me buy you a drink and join you.'

He hadn't lowered his voice at all and Sara could almost feel the ears pricking up around her. She gave him the standard brush-off. 'Sorry, I'm waiting for my boy-friend.'

The man looked at her indignantly, then took himself off and the chatter resumed around her. But now there weren't any more speculative looks. As long as they thought she had a man somewhere around it was all right; they knew where they stood and accepted her as one of them. It was all so darn hypocritical that it made her clench her teeth in anger and after five minutes she threw down the magazine and walked out. Whether Nicky had finished her cosy chat or not, she wasn't going to hang around any longer.

# CHAPTER FIVE

It was after nine when Sara pulled into the driveway of Appleberry and parked the car alongside Alex's Aston Martin. She noticed that the reflector had been replaced and a slight dent in the wing straightened out. She must remember to ask him how much it cost so that she could pay him. She certainly didn't intend to be in debt to him, she thought grimly. As she locked the car, the front door opened and Alex came out and down the steps.

'It's all right, I didn't scratch your car when I parked,' she said tartly.

He came towards her, his hands in his pockets. 'I see you're in your usual charming mood. Where did you get the car?'

'Hired it from the local garage. They'll collect it in the morning.'

She went to walk past him, but he said, 'Don't go in yet; I want to talk to you. Come for a walk in the garden.'

Sara hesitated for a moment, then shrugged and followed him round the side of the house. He strolled over to a wooden garden seat and sat down, his legs stretched out as usual and his hands still in his pockets. Sara had, perforce, to sit down beside him.

'Well?' she asked impatiently.

'I had a long talk with Richard today.'

'And?' Sara prompted when he didn't immediately

go on. 'Did you make him see sense and persuade him to give up this crazy idea?'

Alex took out his cigarette case and offered her one, but she shook her head. When he had lit his own, he went on, 'Richard's a quiet sort of chap. He doesn't usually show his feelings very much and he's certainly never shown much interest in girls before, but he told me that he's very fond of Nicky and he thinks they'll get along okay together.'

'Fond? Is that all?'

Alex grinned slightly. 'For Richard that's a lot. He isn't the type to go completely overboard for a girl, but I think he really cares about Nicky. And now he's found her he doesn't see any point in not getting married. He's sorry that you don't approve, of course, but he's quite determined about it.'

'And you? What do you think?'

Alex drew on his cigarette and answered slowly. 'I must admit that I have a grudging admiration for him. To be willing to take on the responsibilities of marriage at his age requires a kind of courage and....'

'Or crass stupidity,' Sara broke in angrily.

'Perhaps. But the fact remains that they both know what they want. By withholding your consent you're only postponing the inevitable by a few months anyway.'

'In which time either of them could very easily have grown out of it,' Sara pointed out.

'I don't think they will,' he replied shortly. 'I think this is for keeps.'

'Am I to take it that you're in favour of this—this silly teenage crush, then?'

Alex's jaw tightened. 'You can take it that I am no longer against it, yes.'

Sara stood up and glared at him hostilely. 'And just

what are they supposed to live on? Answer me that.'

'Richard's parents aren't very well off, admittedly, but his father manages to send him a small allowance every month, they'll have to manage on that, I suppose. Unless you come to your senses and let Nicky have her money now when she needs it most,' he said coolly.

His calmness only served to increase her anger. 'So that's what they sent you out here for, was it? To try and talk me into letting them have the money. Well, it won't work, because there's no way I'm going to let Nicky squander it. The time she'll really need it is when *she* comes to her senses and wants to get a divorce and pick up the pieces again.' Her voice rose furiously. 'I won't give way to Nicky, whatever she accuses me of, and I....'

'Is that why you hit her, because she called you a few names? Told you a few home truths?' Alex interrupted suddenly. He was still sitting casually on the seat, but there was a grim, hard look to his mouth, a tenseness in his shoulders.

'Oh, she told you that, did she? She was almost hysterical and I....'

'Really?' Alex stood up and loomed over her so that for a second Sara felt as if she was facing some predatory animal about to strike. 'But she wasn't completely hysterical, was she? Just enough to give you the excuse to take your feelings out on her. You seem to like hitting people who antagonise you. First me, and now Nicky. Maybe it's about time somebody started slapping you around for a change.'

Sara stared at him and said unsteadily, 'Like you, for instance, I suppose?'

'Like me, for instance.' His hands came out and gripped her by the arms, tightening cruelly when she tried to get away. His mouth curled derisively. 'But you'd like that, wouldn't you? Using brute force would never subdue you, just give you another reason for hating me. But maybe there's another way to get through to you.'

He drew her to him suddenly and his mouth closed on hers, his arms imprisoning her as he kissed her with a fierce, bruising intensity. At first she tried to break free, but his strong arms held her close against him and her struggles only seemed to increase the brutality of his embrace. So instead she stood rigidly, feeling his lips warm and searching on hers, feeling his body hard against her own, aware of the sensations he was arousing in her but fighting them down.

When he raised his head at last, her eyes blazed up at him. 'You snake! Take your hands off me! I should have known you were the type to....'

But that was as far as she got before he again covered her mouth with his, and by the time he let her go this time she was quivering with something other than rage. Slowly she raised her eyes and gazed at his face, shadowed in the darkness. He was watching her with almost detached interest to see what her reaction would be, a slight curl of derisive amusement on his lips. A feeling of cold rage filled her as she looked at him. To him it was all a game, a way to amuse himself while stuck out here in the country. He would enjoy bringing her to heel, and the fact that she had disliked him on sight and hadn't hesitated to let him know it would make his victory all the sweeter. Well, two could play at that game.

Lifting her chin, she said disdainfully, 'And just what was *that* supposed to prove? Did you really think that a couple of kisses was going to make me change my

mind? What was I supposed to do—fall head over heels
in love with your rather obvious charms? Well, I've
news for you, Alex Brandon; as a lover you don't even
make the third grade! You might turn on a kid of
Nicky's age with that big he-man act, but I advise you
not to try it on a grown woman unless you want her to
laugh in your face!'

And with that she turned and hurried back to the
house, her ears alert for sounds of him following her.
But there were none, so at the corner she felt it safe to
glance back. Alex was bending his head to light another
cigarette, then he straightened and began to walk
slowly down through the garden towards the lake. Sara
gave a sigh of relief and hoped fervently that she had
squashed any ideas he might have of trying that tactic
again, because she knew, with terrifying certainty, that
that was one area in which she would never be able to
fight him. From the moment his lips had touched hers
she had felt herself powerless against his masculine
strength and dominance. It was knowledge that frightened her because she had never before been in a situation she couldn't control. Well, for a few days longer
she would have to put up with his company, and she
would make darn sure that it never happened again,
she resolved grimly as she turned to go inside.

But those few moments in the garden had changed
the whole pattern of their relationship. Sara was fully
aware of Alex now as a man—and he knew it too, as
she found out when she came down to breakfast the
next morning and found him drinking coffee and chatting to Mrs Ogden. Deliberately he ran his eyes slowly
down her slim figure and then up again to look her
directly in the eyes. She lifted her chin and tried to stare
back at him defiantly, but despite her efforts she felt

herself flushing beneath his insolent gaze. Then he smiled, a slow sardonic smile that spoke volumes and left her feeling angry and dispirited. She turned her back on him while she prepared a couple of slices of toast, but the damage was done; she knew now that she had given him a weapon to use against her, and she had no doubts that he wouldn't hesitate to do so just as soon as she tried to cross him again.

That day she took care to keep out of his way, staying in the kitchen to help Mrs Ogden as much as she could. At lunch time Veronica came down and this helped to ease the strained atmosphere round the table. Sara realised that Nicky had decided to completely ignore her, and poor Richard looked so unhappy about it all that she almost felt sorry for him. Alex spoke to her politely, but there was an undercurrent of mockery in his tone that continually reminded her that their particular battle wasn't over yet.

'I'll take the coffee in, Mrs Ogden,' she offered after she had brought the dishes into the kitchen.

'I'm afraid it isn't brewed yet. I always forget it takes longer when it's full.'

The two women chatted together for the ten minutes or so it took the old coffee pot to finish percolating and then Sara carried the tray along to the drawing-room, her sandals making little noise on the carpeted floor. The door of the drawing-room was slightly ajar and as she went to push it fully open with her elbow, Sara caught her own name being spoken heatedly in Nicky's voice.

'Talking to Sara won't be any use, I tell you. She just ticks you off and tells you it's all for your own good.'

'Then we'll just have to find some other means of convincing her, won't we?' Alex's voice broke in firmly.

'Perhaps it would be best if I talked to her,' Veronica's softer tones joined the conversation. 'Sara really isn't as obstinate as you think. It's just that she doesn't want Nicky to go through the same unhappy experience that she had when she was about Nicky's age. You see she. . . .'

Hastily Sara pushed open the door and carried the tray across to a table, setting it down with a bang. You could have cut the sudden silence with a knife. Richard, his face brilliant red, began to talk quickly to cover it up. 'Oh, coffee, good. I'm really thirsty, aren't you, Nicky?'

He nudged Nicky in the ribs and she said obediently, 'Yes, I am.'

Veronica and Alex handled the situation more diplomatically, but it was obvious that Veronica was unhappily wondering if she had heard.

Outwardly calm, Sara poured the coffee and handed round the cups. To her annoyance a little slopped in the saucer as she handed Alex his. He took the cup but caught her hand before she could draw it away. 'Hand shaking, Sara?' he asked softly.

She opened her mouth to make a sharp retort, but then remembered the others in the room so merely gave him a fiery look before pulling her hand away.

Richard and Nicky drank their coffee as quickly as possible and hurriedly excused themselves. Sara waited for Alex to do the same so that she would be left alone with Veronica, but he seemed in no hurry, chatting on a number of topics and having a second cup of coffee before at last rising to his feet. 'I promised Mrs Ogden that I'd take her into town to do some shopping today. Would you like to come along, Veronica? Sara?'

'I'm afraid I'm not quite up to that yet, Alex. But

Sara must go by all means,' Veronica replied with her usual smile.

'No, thanks. I'll stay and keep you company.'

When he'd gone, Sara said immediately, 'I believe you want to talk to me?'

'Oh dear, so you did overhear,' the older woman sighed. 'I'm sorry if you thought us rude, my dear, but you see I'm afraid I agree with Nicky on this. I think marriage to Richard is just what she needs.'

'And because you've come down on their side you think I ought to change my mind too, is that it?'

'Yes, I do.' Veronica's voice was surprisingly firm. 'You can't base Nicky's future on your past. Just because a man let you down it doesn't mean that Richard will do the same. And what good will withholding your consent do? If you force Nicky to go back to school she won't be able to settle to any work now, and as soon as she's eighteen she'll marry him anyway. And you'll just have destroyed her feelings for you in the process,' she finished.

'Feelings for me?' Sara said in surprise. 'Nicky doesn't have any. She never has had. All I am is a source of clothes and pocket money and a damn nuisance when she can't get her own way. Just like a parent, in fact,' she added mirthlessly. 'And what if they wake up one morning and find it was all a big mistake? What then?'

'I don't think they will. I think they're genuinely in love with one another.'

'You *think* they are. Alex *thinks* they are. But nobody *knows* for sure, do they? This love thing—you think it's happened to you and for a while everything's wonderful, but then something happens to kill it or else it just fades away into a nothingness. I'm not completely inexperienced, Veronica. I've felt like that a dozen times, but it never lasts,' Sara finished on a note of bitterness.

Veronica's hand reached across and touched hers gently. 'That's because the right man hasn't come along for you yet. But he will, and it will be different from anything you've ever felt before, believe me. You've had to wait, but with Nicky it's come almost too soon. *But she knows.* And you will too, one day.'

Sara looked at her frowningly for a long moment, but then slowly shook her head. 'I'm sorry, Veronica, it's a risk I'm not prepared to take. I can't stop her marrying him in September, but until then she goes back to school,' she said determinedly.

When the others came back she kept out of their way, let them have their conferences, talk about her if they wanted to. She was getting tired of the whole thing, and was worried about taking more time off from her job. Making up her mind, Sara decided that she would leave on Saturday and take Nicky straight back to school. There was no point in staying here any longer, it was only prolonging the agony and upsetting Veronica into the bargain.

She had intended getting Nicky to herself and telling her this the next morning, but they were woken early by Alex banging on their bedroom door. 'Come on, you two, it's a beautiful day and we're going sailing. Breakfast in half an hour!'

Sara yawned and looked across at Nicky who was trying to get her eyes open. 'Did you know about this?'

The younger girl shook her head owlishly. 'No. Do you think he means it?'

'Yes, I'm rather afraid he does,' Sara sighed. 'Come on, it looks as if we're going to be Butlinised today.'

But surprisingly she enjoyed the day spent on the sailing dinghy that Alex had hired on Lake Windermere. At first they made a complete hash of things and had to have the correct rope put into their hands by Alex who, it turned out, was a keen sailor and had his own boat at Bucklers Hard. Richard had been out with him a few times so wasn't a complete novice, but both Nicky and Sara came in for a few scathing comments as they hopelessly tangled up the sail or nearly got knocked overboard by the boom. For a while it gave them the common bond of helpless females against experienced males and for once there was no friction between them when they went to a pub for one of the huge 'batch' sandwiches popular in the area.

Alex sat next to her at the table and after he had eaten put a casual arm across the back of her chair. His fingers touched her shoulder and she immediately sat forward, but not until he had felt her involuntary quiver. She felt him looking at her, but didn't turn her head. She didn't have to; she could imagine well enough the coolly sardonic smile that would be on his face.

After lunch they took the boat out again and this time managed to sail the thing up and down the width of the water quite creditably. At about four they took it back to the boatyard and then walked towards the car park.

'Don't you ever wear a skirt?' Alex asked suddenly, and Sara turned to see him regarding her bottom half in the tight jeans with a frown.

Before she could make an indignant retort, Nicky surprisingly answered for her. 'Of course she does! She has some gorgeous clothes, really dreamy.'

'Good. Then she can wear something gorgeous tonight, and so can you. I've booked a table at a hotel in

Keswick for dinner. It's a sort of thank-you to Veronica for putting up with us all.'

Sara looked at him questioningly. 'Is she well enough to go?'

'She says she feels up to it, and if she feels tired we can always cut the evening short and take her home.'

So Sara found herself putting on a long black dress that evening and combing her hair straight back from her head into a tight whorl at the back. Earrings, high-heeled black sandals, make-up; the girl who looked back at her from the mirror looked sophisticated and confident enough to deal with any situation, any man.

Nicky kept most of her clothes at Appleberry and had put on a pretty, layered dress with an inch or two of false petticoat showing at the hem. It suited her and made her look softer, although she had overdone her make-up a bit. Thinking of the evening ahead, Sara wisely forbore mentioning this and went to see if Veronica was ready. She was, and had put on a long dress of pale blue that matched her eyes and showed up the sparkle in them.

'I'm so looking forward to this evening,' she remarked as Sara helped her on with her coat. 'It's done me a world of good having you all here, feeling a part of things again.'

The men were waiting for them at the bottom of the stairs and Sara stared back at Alex as his eyes slid over her appraisingly. She wouldn't let him throw her, she thought fiercely, not tonight. Because tomorrow was Saturday, and tomorrow she was leaving here and taking Nicky with her.

They were shown to a well-placed table in the hotel restaurant, its subdued lighting giving an intimate atmosphere to the tables and small dance floor. A group with a good beat played softly at one end of the room and a blonde vocalist in a tight-fitting dress sang one of the latest hit songs in a throaty voice. Nicky was full of excitement and Veronica was pleased when she was greeted by some acquaintances nearby, so the evening seemed about to be a success right from the start.

The food was good and well served and Alex kept everyone's glass topped up with wine—or would have done if Sara had let him, but when he went to refill Nicky's for the second time, she said sarcastically, 'It may just have slipped your mind, of course, but Nicky is under age.'

'A couple of glasses of wine won't do her any harm,' he replied easily.

'It's against the law.'

'So why don't you call the police?' And he filled up the glass Nicky held out to him.

Nicky turned back to her. 'Don't be a stick-in-the-mud, Sara! All the girls at school have wine when they go out.'

Angrily Sara sat back in her chair and twisted the stem of her own glass between her fingers. Damn the man; he set out to undermine what little hold she had over Nicky at every turn. And enjoyed doing it, too, she thought viciously. Deliberately provoking her when he knew she couldn't make a scene. Lord, she'd be glad when tomorrow came and she got away from him; away from his conceit and autocracy, away from his strength and masculinity, but most of all away from her physical awareness of him every time she was in the same room. As if he read her thoughts, Alex's hand came to cover hers on the table. Sara stared down at it for a moment and felt herself begin to tremble as she felt the warmth of his hand. Slowly she raised her head to find his dark eyes watching her, a strange light deep in their depths that she couldn't read.

'Would you like to dance, Sara?' he asked quietly.

'What?' She had been so deep in thought that she hadn't noticed that Nicky and Richard had left the table and were already dancing. 'Oh. No.' She shook her head.

'Go along, Sara,' Veronica urged her. 'I'm going to call Mrs Smithson over for a chat, so you don't have to worry about me.'

'But I don't want to....' Sara began, but wasn't allowed to finish because Alex had stood up and was pulling her to her feet.

The dance floor was only pocket handkerchief-sized and it was already rather crowded, so that Alex had some excuse in drawing her close to him and holding her hand against his broad chest.

'Why did you do that?' Sara asked tartly. 'You know I don't want to dance with you.' She tried to push herself away from him, but he wouldn't let her, holding her tightly and looking down at her tauntingly.

'Because I wasn't going to have you spoil Veronica's evening. And for that reason you could try to look as if you're enjoying yourself—or is it against the law to smile?' Sara glared at him and didn't bother to answer, deliberately looking at the other dancers. 'By the way,' Alex went on, 'I forgot to tell you, you look very lovely tonight.'

Her eyes came up to meet his, disconcerted by this sudden change. The suspicion in her face made him give an amused chuckle. 'What's the matter? Does a compliment usually mean that a man intends to make a pass at you?'

'In your case it probably means that you're about to

say something extremely rude to counteract it,' she retorted.

He laughed then, his eyes alight with amusement.
'You know, Sara, if you ever wake up to the fact that
you're a woman and get yourself a man, you may drive
him to distraction—but he'll never be bored!'

The music changed just then to a quick tempo number so she was able to free herself from his arms and
dance apart, moving sensuously to the beat. He moved
to the rhythm well, she noticed, nothing flamboyant,
but he wasn't embarrassed to let his hair down a little
and enjoy the music. When they returned to the table,
Veronica introduced them to her friends and told them
that they had offered her a lift home.

'So I won't have to make you young people leave
early when you're enjoying yourselves,' she added cheer-
fully.

'That really isn't necessary. We'll be glad to take you
now if you're tired,' Sara assured her.

But Veronica was quite adamant that they should
stay on and in face of her determination Sara had to
reluctantly agree. As Sara turned from saying goodbye
she found Alex watching her derisively and she bit her
lip; he knew full well she had wanted to leave now because she was afraid to spend more time in his close
company.

Richard took Nicky off to dance again and Alex
filled her glass with more wine. 'How did you enjoy
your sailing lesson today?' he asked casually.

'More than I expected,' she admitted. 'It would probably be fun once you got the hang of it and could go
out on the open sea.'

'You'd have to have a lot more practice first. Why

don't we take a boat out again on Sunday and I'll give you another lesson?'

For a fleeting moment Sara wondered if the 'we' included Nicky and Richard, but it didn't really matter now. 'Thanks,' she said clearly, 'but I won't be here on Sunday. I've decided to take Nicky back to school tomorrow.'

Alex stared at her for a minute, his glass poised in his hand, then he set it down with a snap, spilling a little of the wine so that it spread in a blood-red pool on the whiteness of the tablecloth. 'Just like that?' he said grimly. 'You're going to ignore everyone else involved and drag Nicky back to school just as if nothing had happened. What if she refuses to go?'

'Then I shall have to have her made a ward of court,' Sara replied coolly.

'With all the attendant publicity that such a move would invite? What sort of life do you think she'd have at school after that? The other girls would make her life a misery.'

'She should have thought of that before she ran away.' Deliberately she kept her voice hard.

Alex looked at her contemptuously. 'I think Nicky was right about you, after all; you don't like her.'

'Of course I like her. She's my sister, isn't she?'

'Well, you certainly don't love her,' he returned caustically, 'or you wouldn't be putting her through all this.'

Sara was about to reply when the music stopped and she turned away angrily as the youngsters returned. What was the use of arguing with the man? He'd never understand.

They stayed at the restaurant for an hour or so longer and she danced with Alex twice more, but only to the fast numbers where they could dance without touching, without speaking. The atmosphere between them was strained, and the tension must have communicated itself to the younger couple because they too were subdued and raised no demur when Alex suggested it was time they left. Sara went into the cloakroom to get her coat and as she came out saw the three of them with their heads together as Richard and Nicky listened to something that Alex was saying. Whatever it was he broke off immediately he saw her, and Sara flushed angrily. She was getting good and tired of everyone talking about her behind her back as if she was some sort of criminal!

She sat in stony silence on the journey home and gave a sigh of relief when they pulled into the circular driveway of Appleberry. Leaning down, she groped for the catch of her safety belt, hearing the back doors slam as Nicky and Richard got out. Then suddenly they were moving again and Alex was driving out into the lane and accelerating fast down the road.

'What on earth?' Sara hastily replaced the safety belt. 'Why are you driving on? Where are you going?' she asked in amazement.

'Somewhere where we can talk. I've got a great deal to say to you,' Alex replied grimly, his mouth a set line in his hard face.

'Well, you can just turn round and go right back again, because I've listened to just about as much as I can take from you. Do you hear me? Stop the car and go back!'

Alex's knuckles tightened on the wheel but apart from that he took absolutely no notice, sending the car speeding along the lane. Enraged, Sara reached over and pulled the key out of the ignition. The car jerked

as if it had been kicked and swerved sickeningly before
Alex pushed the clutch in hard and braked to a stand-
still.

'You little bitch, you could have killed us both! Give
me those keys!' he said furiously.

'Not until you promise to take me straight back.'

'When I'm good and ready. Now, are you going to
give me those keys or do you want me to take them
from you?' he asked, his voice dangerous. 'And don't
get any fancy ideas about putting them down the front
of your dress, because I'll get them from there, too, if
I have to. In fact I'd quite enjoy doing it,' he added
nastily.

Sara stared at him balefully. 'I bet you would! Well,
you're not going to get the chance.' She turned quickly
and opened the door, raising her hand to throw the
keys out into the bushes, but Alex moved so swiftly
that she had no time, catching her wrist and pulling
the door shut again. There was a brief, unequal
struggle. She tried to claw at him, but he caught her
arm and pinned it down.

'You wildcat! Give me those keys,' he demanded
harshly, and when she wouldn't let go, twisted her wrist
cruelly. For a few moments she held out against him,
biting her lip against the pain, but then he twisted
again and she gave a little choking cry as she opened her
hand and the key ring fell on to her lap.

Alex picked it up quickly, hardly glancing at her
averted face before restarting the car, straightening it
and driving on. He drove for a couple of miles further
until they were past Lowmere village and away from
any houses, but Sara hardly noticed where they were
going as she sat, back ramrod-straight and seething with
anger at being forced to do what he wanted. They came

to a gravelled track that led down to a clearing on the
edge of a lake and here Alex parked, turning off the
engine and being careful to put the keys in his pocket.

'*Now* we'll talk,' he told her grimly.

'Talk to yourself. There's nothing you can say that
will interest me.' Sara opened the door and got out,
slamming it hard. The moon had gone behind a cloud
and it was very dark and cold. She shivered and pulled
her thin coat more closely around her. Damn Alex
Brandon! She wasn't going to stay in his tyrannical
company another minute, even if she had to walk all
the way back to Appleberry.

He let her get almost back to the road before he came
after her and brought her back, struggling futilely. He
pushed her back against the side of the car and held
her there, his chest heaving as he recovered his breath.

'You're going to listen to me, Sara, if I have to keep
you here all night,' he said savagely. 'And we're going
to forget this thing between us that makes you turn
every encounter into a battlefield. That will have to
be settled one way or another, but not now. Now you're
going to think of nothing but Nicky; her future and
her happiness.' His hand came up to cup her chin. 'Do
you understand?'

Sara glared at him and his hand slid down to her
throat, tightening perceptibly. Hastily she nodded and
he loosened his hand a little. 'All right. So you want to
talk—go ahead. You've got yourself a captive audience,
haven't you?' she said bitterly.

He looked at her angrily, his eyes blazing, but then
his expression changed, a strange look passed over his
lean face and his mouth twisted. 'My God, how I wish
that...!' He broke off abruptly and stepped back away
from her, running his hand through his dishevelled

hair. He hesitated for a moment, then said in a very different voice, 'Sara, you've seen Richard and Nicky together all day, first sailing and then at the restaurant. They were happy together, surely you could see that?'

'Is that what this whole day was for, then? Just to show me that they enjoyed each other's company?' she asked incredulously.

'Partly.'

'And the other part?'

His eyes were very dark as they stared into hers. 'I told you—that comes later.'

Sara's heart gave a sudden, dizzying lurch and then began to pound so loudly that she could hear it. Determinedly she forced herself not to think about the implications behind his remark and concentrated only on the matter in hand. 'Just watching them cooing all over one another isn't going to make me change my mind, Alex. The answer's still no.'

'All right. Then we do it the hard way.' He stuck his hands in his pockets and said coldly, 'I'd hoped to save you from this, Sara, but you leave me no alternative.'

She looked at him in bewilderment. 'What do you mean?'

'I mean that you've no choice. You've *got* to give them your permission.'

'Oh, have I? And just what makes you think I'm. . . .'

'Because they *have* to get married. Just as soon as it can be arranged.'

Sara could only stare at him numbly, the import of his harsh words sinking into her brain in spite of an inner voice that cried, 'No, no, it can't be true!'

In curiously detached tones she said slowly, 'You mean that Nicky's. . .?'

'I mean that they've anticipated the marriage service,

yes.' There was no sympathy in his voice, nothing to alleviate the hurt he had inflicted.

'But she told me she hadn't.... That they hadn't....' Desperately she sought for some means of disproving what he'd told her.

'It doesn't matter what they said. The fact is that you've got to give your permission so that they can get married at once.'

His cold matter-of-factness seemed to trigger something inside Sara and she suddenly began to cry, turning to beat her fists against the roof of the car in her distress. 'Oh, no. No! She's hardly more than a child herself. The silly, stupid little idiot! She's thrown it all away, everything her father worked for, everything her mother sacrificed for her!' She found that Alex had somehow come and turned her round, drawn her towards him, but she pulled herself sharply away to stand facing him, tears pouring unheeded down her cheeks. 'She could have had it all; an education, a degree, met the right people, learned how to behave. She could have walked into any job she wanted instead of having to claw and fight every step of the way. Wouldn't have had to take insults and innuendoes, wouldn't have had to watch the man she loved being slowly twisted by jealousy because she was better at the job than he was....' Sara put her hands up to hide her face, racked with sobs.

'Sara.' Alex took her into his arms again and held her close, but she angrily tried to push him away.

'Leave me alone! I don't need you. I don't need anyone!'

'Oh, yes, you do, Sara. You may not even know it yourself, but right now you need a masculine shoulder to cry on.'

For a few minutes she leant against him, feeling the strength and hardness of his chest beneath her head, smelling the tang of his woody aftershave, his arms warm and protective around her. It would have been so easy just to let go and cry away her shock and unhappiness, turn to him and let him comfort her, to give in completely to the role he expected of her. Resolutely she straightened and stepped away from him, head up, sniffing hard, and using her fingers to wipe away the tears.

'There's just one thing I want to know,' she said unsteadily, clenching her teeth as she strove to control her emotions. 'Why you? Why were you the one to tell me and not Nicky herself?'

His arms dropped to his sides and he shrugged slightly. 'I should have thought that was obvious. Nicky was afraid to tell you and Richard you would have intimidated completely. And Veronica, of course, isn't well enough. So as I'm the only one who isn't afraid of you, it was left to me to bear the brunt.'

'I see.' Turning away from him, Sara walked down to the water's edge and stood, a slight, dark figure against the blackness of the night. Gradually she became aware of the night sounds around her, the rustles in the reed beds and the slight popping sound as a fish came up momentarily to catch an insect on the surface. An owl hooted far away as the full moon slid from behind a cloud and gave a ghostlike appearance to the scene. For a long time she stood there, oblivious to the creeping chilliness, slowly assimilating the bitter knowledge that she had failed; failed to carry out her dead parents' wishes, failed to keep Nicky safe from harm, and, in a way, had failed Nicky too, in that the girl had felt unable to confide in her when she was in trouble. She had tried to take the place of Nicky's parents, worked for her

and been grateful for every success because it had meant
that her sister could have trips abroad with the school
and everything else she needed. But it hadn't been
enough, and it had all gone wrong, so wrong. They were
further apart now than strangers and Nicky had turned
to others for the help it should have been Sara's right
to give. The sense of her own failure filled her heart
with bitterness and self-contempt. It seemed as if she
was incapable of ever holding the affections of those
she loved; first her mother, then her ex-fiancé, and now
Nicky. The wall that she had started to build round
her grew then and turned to ice.

Turning, she walked back to Alex Brandon who was
leaning against the car, smoking a cigarette, and said in
a voice that was just as cold, 'Would you take me back
now, please?'

He stubbed out the cigarette and went to open the
door for her, but she opened it herself and got in before
he could do so. When he was sitting in the seat alongside, he hesitated before starting the engine. 'Have you
made up your mind what you're going to do, Sara?'

Without looking at him she said steadily, 'I'd rather
not talk now, if you don't mind. I have a headache.'

'Look, Sara, this has to be settled once and for all.
You can't just leave. . . .'

Swiftly she turned her head to look at him, her eyes
over-bright. 'As you said; I have no choice. So now that
you've got what you wanted, will you please take me
back to Appleberry?'

He seemed about to speak but changed his mind and
drove them home in a tense silence. As soon as they got
to the house Sara let herself in and went straight upstairs without saying goodnight. Frowningly Alex stood
in the hall and watched her go.

Usually she was careful with her clothes, hanging

them up or folding them neatly away, but tonight she just let them lie where they fell, hurrying into her nightdress, instinctively aware that Nicky's figure in the other bed was too obviously still, that she was only pretending to be asleep. So Sara lay there, a houseful of people all around her, and knew that she had never felt so alone in all her life.

# CHAPTER SIX

SARA supposed that she must have dozed a little during the long night, but when she crept out of bed at six the next morning, just as the greyness of dawn appeared through the windows, she felt as tired and wretched as if she hadn't slept at all. Careful not to wake Nicky, she went to the bathroom and then pulled the curtains aside to look out. It was raining, the drops pattering against the windowpanes and filling the puddles that had already formed in the driveway. She shivered and quickly pulled a thick sweater over her head and put her legs into the warmth of a pair of cord jeans. She hurried over her hair and make-up, then glanced at her watch. Not yet seven; still too early to phone the garage for a car to take her to the station to catch a train to London. Quickly she packed her clothes into her suitcase, pushing them in anyhow, obsessed with the wish to get away from here as soon as possible.

As quietly as she could she carried her case and bag downstairs and left them in the front porch with her jacket, then she went to Veronica's study and sat down at the writing desk. Her first letter was very business-like; in it she gave her permission for Nicky to marry Richard French and addressed it to whoever it might concern. The second letter was to Veronica and was harder to write, because she was very fond of Nicky's godmother and disliked going off without saying good-bye to her personally, but there was no way in which she was going to hang around here until Veronica felt

123

like getting up or seeing her. The thought of writing
to Nicky crossed her mind but was instantly dismissed;
there was nothing she could do for her sister now other
than the step she had already taken of breaking the tie
between them completely.

She sealed down the envelope to Veronica, but left
the other one open, and propped them up on the
mantelpiece where they might easily be seen. It was
seven-thirty and she thought there might be someone
at the garage by now, so she went out into the hall and
dialled the number. After a longish wait a cheerful
voice answered and promised to send a car as soon as he
could.

'Thank you. I'll be waiting.' She put the phone down
and turned to go into the kitchen. As she did so she saw
Alex standing at the top of the stairs. Sara ignored him,
but he ran lightly down and followed her into the
kitchen.

'That was a rather early call, wasn't it? Who were
you phoning?' he asked abruptly.

Picking up the kettle, Sara filled it and plugged it in
before she turned to face him. He looked as if he had
got dressed in a hurry, his dark hair was dishevelled
and he was wearing navy slacks and a matching V-
necked sweater without a shirt. The sleeves he had
pushed up and this somehow made him appear even
more strong and implacable.

'I'm making coffee, do you want some?'

'No, I want to know who you were phoning. Are you
up to something, because if you are I'll. . . .'

'You'll find my written consent to the marriage in
Veronica's study,' Sara interrupted him coldly.

Alex looked at her for long seconds, but she returned
his gaze steadily, unemotionally, until he walked

abruptly away towards the study. Sara made herself a mug of coffee and sat down at the kitchen table to drink it, the fiery liquid warming and reviving her a little. When he came back he was holding both her letters in his hand, the letter of consent he had taken out and read.

'This letter to Veronica,' he said, dropping it in front of her. 'I take it it's by way of saying goodbye?'

Silently she nodded.

'And I suppose that phone call was for a car?'

'Yes.'

He came to sit on the edge of the table, looking down at her contemptuously. 'And Nicky? Have you no letter to leave for her?'

'Nicky and I have nothing to say to each other,' she replied with only the slightest tremor in her voice.

'Did you talk to her last night when we got back?' he asked sharply.

'No, she pretended to be asleep.'

'And now you're going off without a word to her,' he said sneeringly. 'I've thought you all sorts of things, Sara, but I've never thought you were a coward until now.'

Sara's face hardened and she gripped the mug tightly.

'Whatever you may think, Sara, Nicky needs you now. She's a young girl just entering into marriage and she'll need the advice and help of an older woman to give her confidence, guide her.'

'She has Veronica for all that.'.

'Not Veronica, Sara, you. Someone she can turn to when she needs a friend, a confidant....'

'Aren't you getting a bit mixed up?' she asked sarcastically. 'When Nicky wanted someone to confide in she went to Veronica and you, not me. And you seem to be forgetting that she knows it all already, or else she wouldn't be in this mess. And as for me—why, I'm just a career-minded spinster, that's all.'

A muscle tightened in Alex's jaw, but he went on, 'Now that you've given your permission they'll be able to get a special licence and be married in just a few days. Surely you can stay until then?'

'No.' Sara finished her coffee and took the mug over to the sink to wash.

Alex came and stood close behind her. 'Sara, I know that you've been hurt, far more than I ever thought you could be—last night proved that—but won't you give Nicky even the chance to tell you she's sorry, ask you to forgive her?'

Blindly she looked down at the mug in her hands. Forgive Nicky? When she was so much aware that it ought to be the other way around! Slowly she shook her head. 'There's nothing to forgive,' she said indistinctly.

'And us?' His voice was suddenly harsh. 'Are you going to run away from what's between us, as well?'

With an unsteady hand she put the mug on the draining-board and turned round to face him. He was standing very close, his eyes cold and steely in his grim face. 'There's nothing between us,' she said firmly.

His eyes narrowed. 'There is and you know it.'

'No, I don't. It's just something you've built up in your imagination. You can't bear to think that I don't fancy you, so you've convinced yourself that I'm hiding a. . . .'

'Don't you? Don't you really, Sara? Then why is it that you tremble whenever I touch you?' he asked softly. Very deliberately he reached out and pulled her against him, his eyes never leaving hers, then he put his hands under her sweater on to the bare skin at the curve of her waist. They felt warm and sensuous as they gently caressed her. She tried to force herself to remain unmoved, but as his hands began to explore further her lips parted and her breathing quickened.

Hurriedly she stepped back until brought up short by the sink. 'All right! So I admit you're capable of turning me on, but it's only basic chemistry, nothing more. And it certainly isn't strong enough to keep me here,' she added in a rush, disgusted with herself for letting him see how easily he could make her respond.

'Don't lie to me, Sara. This is more than that and you know it as well as I do. It's been there from the start. You've been antagonistic towards me right from the beginning because you felt this and tried to fight it. But you can't fight any more, Sara. *It's there!* And I'm going to make you face up to it and accept it.'

'Accept you, you mean,' she retorted bitterly.

'That's just what I mean. I want you, Sara.' His eyes glinted down at her, dark and dangerous.

'So what?'

'So—this.' He took a purposeful step towards her as Sara raised her hands in a futile attempt to ward him off, but he merely smiled tartly and caught her wrists, pinioning them to her sides. Briefly she tried to struggle, but he said harshly, 'I've told you, the fight's over. It's too late.' Then, 'Oh, hell, what's the use of talking to you?' He released her wrists and pulled her roughly into his arms. His mouth covered hers hungrily, claiming possession, allowing no resistance. Desperately she tried to break free, twisting her head until his hand came up to twine itself in the thickness of her hair and she could no longer move to escape the passionate torment of his lips, searching, demanding a response. She

made a little sound deep in her throat and the hand
that had been raised to hit him instead sank slowly on
to his shoulder and crept up round his neck. His arm
tightened around her and his kiss became even deeper,
sending the room whirling around and awakening emotions that were new and frightening. At last he raised
his head, loosening his grip a little, but not letting her
go.

Slowly Sara opened her eyes, her lower lip trembling
and sensuous. There was triumph in his face as he
looked down at her, the triumph of mastery, the knowledge that he had won curving his mouth and lighten-
ing his eyes.

'So now we both know what we want,' he said softly.
'Don't we?'

She couldn't bear to see her defeat written in his face
and she looked away, not answering. But he was determined to have complete victory over her, her full submission.

'Don't we?' he said again forcefully, his hand tightening in her hair.

Never before had Sara felt so completely defenceless,
so weak before the indomitable will and sheer mag-
netism of the man who held her. Her mind cried out
to deny his power over her, but her body still felt his
closeness and she was aware of an intense longing to
submit to him, to give herself utterly into his hands.
Raising her eyes, she found him looking at her searchingly. She tried to speak, to whisper yes, but her voice
stuck in her throat. She took a breath and went to try
again.

Dimly she heard the door open behind them and suddenly the broad-accented voice of Mrs Ogden shattered
the silence as she demanded to know what was going

on. Alex swore harshly under his breath and stepped back. Dazedly Sara straightened up and stared at the housekeeper.

'Are you all right, Miss Sara? Ee, you look as white as a sheet!' Then in a whisper, 'Has he been doing something he shouldn't? Because if he has I'll. . . .'

'No, it's all right,' Sara reassured her shakily. 'Is—is that the doorbell? It must be my taxi.'

There followed a confused five minutes until she was actually sitting in the back of the cab. Alex came to shut the door for her. 'I'll look you up as soon as I get back to London,' he said brusquely.

But he was a safe distance away from her now and Sara could function on a sane level again. 'Don't bother. You'll be wasting your time,' she returned curtly.

He smiled derisively. 'You may have been saved by the bell this time, but it isn't over yet. Not by a long chalk!' And then he'd slammed the door and she was at last driving away from his tormenting presence.

At first it felt good to be back in London, in the privacy of her own flat and among the usual crises that cropped up daily in her work. The cosmetics account wanted total coverage in all the women's glossies for a new range of lipstick and Sara had to arrange for the photographic department to take shots of several different approaches for the client to choose from. It was exacting work that demanded her full attention as she set up the different ideas, but somehow she found it difficult to concentrate, couldn't settle down to give her whole mind to the job as she had in the past. Several times she had to pull herself together sharply as someone appealed to her for a decision or asked her a question only to find her gazing abstractedly into space.

Telling herself that she must be tired after all the tensions of the past week, Sara went to bed early, but this only made things worse because she lay awake and thought unhappily of her sister so far away, turning to others for comfort and help. Inevitably her thoughts turned, too, to Alex, but these she pushed resolutely aside. She had had a narrow escape and it had taught her a lesson. She was fully aware that to Alex Brandon she had represented a challenge; he had seen her as a woman who could get along without a man, and this had pricked his male vanity so that he had deliberately set out to break her, to make her admit that she wanted him. And he hadn't only wanted to make her admit it, he had wanted to take her physically, to have her utter capitulation. He wasn't the first man who had tried it, but he was certainly the first who had come anywhere near success, as she honestly admitted. Abstractedly she wondered why it was that a certain type of man resented the fact that a woman could make it on her own, felt the need to exert their masculinity until they beat you into submission. But at least she'd managed to get away from Alex before he'd won that particular battle, she thought with relief. But still the thoughts kept coming back to haunt her days and to keep her awake at nights. Restlessly she pummelled the pillows and tried to sleep, but it was no good; the memories were there inside her and couldn't be shut out however hard she tried.

Soon after she got back a letter arrived in Nicky's unformed hand. It wasn't very long and Sara could guess at the difficulty her sister had had in writing it. In it Nicky first thanked her for her consent and told her the date and time of the wedding. Then she went on:

'We're going to be married in the church at Lowmere and Veronica has bought me a dress as a wedding present. I know you're terribly angry with me, Sara, and I don't suppose you'll *ever* forgive me, but I *do* wish you'd come to the wedding. After all, you are my sister. And *Richard* would like you to come too.' Nicky was at an age to enjoy underlining, Sara noted.

Without giving herself time to think about it, she immediately wrote back saying that she would be unable to attend and enclosed a cheque for a hundred pounds as a wedding present. This brought two replies which arrived on the same day; the first a stilted note from Richard thanking her for the gift, the second an extremely terse directive from Alex Brandon: 'If you don't come there won't be any wedding. As the consenting guardian you have to sign the certificate.'

Sara looked at this last letter in consternation. The last thing she wanted to do was to see him again so soon, and she had no wish to see Nicky tied in a marriage that she was sure would turn out to be a disaster. Suspiciously she got her secretary to check his facts, but as far as they could find out it seemed that Alex was right and that she had no alternative but to attend. She bit her lip in vexation, then took herself roundly to task. Was she so afraid of the man that she couldn't spend a few hours in his company without going to pieces? And those surrounded by other people? It took a lot of this kind of talk before she could bring herself to pick up the phone and tell them she was coming, and in the end she chickened out and told Jane, her secretary, to do it for her, because she knew in her heart she was afraid Alex might answer the phone.

Her car had been repaired while she was away and delivered back to the firm's garage, so she was able to

set out very early on the Saturday of the wedding and
get well up the motorway before the traffic became
heavy and unpleasant. The ceremony wasn't until
three-thirty, so she had plenty of time. Once she overtook a man in a sports car and he immediately tooted
her up and tried to make a race of it, but she resolutely
ignored him and eventually he turned off at a junc-
tion. She didn't want to be late, but even less did she
want to be early, so she stopped at a roadside café for
coffee, timing it so that she pulled into the driveway
of Appleberry at exactly three o'clock.

Surprisingly, there were several cars already there
and among them a caterer's van. Sara reached for the
hat she had brought with her, a round one with a
slightly curled brim, and using the driving mirror to
see her reflection, swept her hair up beneath it. Then
she added a pair of large-lensed dark glasses before she
felt confident enough to face everyone. As she got out
of the car she heard the sound of voices and laughter
coming from the garden, and curiosity overcoming her,
she strolled round to see who it was. There were a few
people, obviously guests, standing in a group, and on
the other side of the garden, sideways on to the lake,
there was an open-fronted marquee where two
waitresses were busily arranging a buffet on damask-
cloth-covered tables. Sara's first feeling was one of
astonishment; because of the shotgun nature of the
marriage she had expected Veronica, Alex and herself
to be the only guests, but it was obvious that quite a
large number were being catered for.

While she was still trying to think who all the guests
could possibly be, a familiar voice behind her said casually, 'Glad you could make it.'

Taking a deep breath before she turned to face him,

she gave a bright, brittle smile. 'Hallo, Alex. How are you?'

His eyebrows rose slightly. 'Fine. And you? Working hard as usual, I expect.'

If he had meant to draw her he didn't succeed. 'Of course. Is Veronica about? I haven't seen her yet.'

'I believe she's in the drawing-room, but I shouldn't disturb her at the moment; she's having ten minutes with her feet up before she goes to the church.' His eyes ran over her appraisingly. 'You look very sophisticated.'

'Do I?' she asked, glancing down at the soft cream woollen blouson suit she was wearing. 'From anyone else I'd probably take that as a compliment.'

His left eyebrow rose interrogatively. 'But not from me?'

Sara smiled sweetly. 'Hardly. You have such strange ideas about the difference between sophistication and self-confidence!' And with this shot she turned on her heel and went to greet Mrs Ogden who had appeared at the back door in her best outfit, looking rather flustered at all the comings and goings. The housekeeper seemed pleased to see her and chattered excitedly on for several minutes before Sara had a chance to ask her how Veronica Quinlan was.

'Oh, very well, Miss Sara. She's done all the phoning, and any running around that's needed to be done, Mr Alex has done it,' she added approvingly. So he had got to Mrs Ogden too, had he? Sara thought drily.

But the wedding cars started arriving then and Alex came to shepherd her into the first one with some people who introduced themselves as relations of the bridegroom. Her high heels made loud clicking noises as she walked the length of the aisle to take her place on the left-hand side of the church. Trust the bride to be put on the left hand, she thought cynically. The church was a small one, built of local stone, and every available surface was filled with vases and arrangements of flowers. The day was fine and bright and the sun shone through the stained glass windows, casting gaily coloured patterns of light on the worn stone slabs of the floor.

Behind her she could hear the pews filling up and presently Richard and Alex came to sit in the front pew on the other side of the aisle. Richard, dressed in a conservative dark suit and with his hair cut shorter, seemed nervous and ill at ease, but Alex talked to him and made him smile at something he said. Suddenly Alex turned his head and looked directly across at her. For a moment she felt completely open and vulnerable, but then remembered she was still wearing the dark glasses and gave an inner sigh of relief. Thank the Lord for modern science!

The organ had been playing quietly in the background, but now it changed to the Wedding March as everyone stood up to await the entrance of the bride. It had never occurred to Sara to wonder who would be giving her away, so it came as something of a shock when she saw Nicky being escorted down the aisle by her godmother, and there was such a look of pride and happiness on Veronica's face that Sara hastily bent her head to look down at her hymn book. She felt a fierce surge of envy run through her. If only she had been able to have such a warm and loving relationship with her sister! The old feelings of bitterness and failure crept like a cold hand round her heart and tears pricked threateningly at the back of her eyes. Defiantly she lifted her chin and began to sing.

At the end of the ceremony all the principal guests

followed the bridal pair into the little vestry to sign the marriage certificate. After Nicky had done so she turned a face up to Richard that was so radiant with happiness that in that moment she was almost beautiful. That the power of love could so transform someone came as something of a shock, especially when Sara saw a now very composed and dignified Richard confidently add his signature and turn round to receive the congratulations of the guests.

'Miss Royle, if you would sign now, please,' the vicar said, indicating the place.

Rather dazedly she stepped forward and fumbled to take off the sun-specs. It took all her control to write her name clearly and as soon as she put down the pen her hand began to shake. Alex stepped quickly forward to add his signature, but then he was beside her, taking the glasses from her as she raised them to put on again.

'You don't need these any more, Sara,' he said softly, and put them into his pocket.

For a long second she gazed up at him, her eyes wide and naked in her pale face, then she turned abruptly and went back to her seat.

Sara kept well in the background at the reception, chatting to the few people she knew, who were mostly friends of Veronica's; the other guests she gathered were mostly Richard's relations and school friends of Nicky's. She kept glancing at her watch, wondering how soon she could decently leave. Veronica had come up to her almost at once with her usual cheery smile.

'I'm so glad you came, my dear. Nicky would have been so upset if you hadn't.'

Sara doubted this very much, but she let it pass. 'I had no idea you were going to have so many people,' she remarked. 'This reception must have cost a bomb, and I should have been the one to provide it. You must promise to send me the bill, Veronica, or better still tell me how much it cost and I'll give you a cheque now,' she added, reaching for her bag.

'But it hasn't cost me a penny, my dear. Alex paid for it all. And do you know, he had the boathouse repaired as a surprise for me. I didn't know anything about it until he took me down there to show me when it was all finished. You must go and see it later.'

'Yes. Yes, I will. But hadn't you better sit down for a while now?' She found the older woman a chair and turned to make way for others who had come up to talk. As she did so she came face to face with Nicky and Richard.

Richard said at once, 'We wanted to thank you properly for your super present, Sara. Didn't we Nicky?' he added, giving his new wife an insistent nudge.

'Yes. It was very generous of you, Sara.' Nicky carefully avoided her eyes, a faint flush of embarrassment on her cheeks.

Sara smiled woodenly. 'The least I could do.' There was a rather strained silence and to break it she said quickly, 'You look very nice. Quite slim and grown up.' The moment she said it she could have bitten out her tongue, but it was too late. Nicky went beetroot red and turned sharply away, Richard following her after he had shot Sara a darkling glance. Biting her lip, Sara cursed herself for being a fool and wished heartily that she could get away from here. But first there was the cake to be cut and the telegrams to be read before Nicky changed and they were at last ready to go off on their honeymoon. Sara overheard a relation of Richard's mention that Alex had given them the car they were to go in as a wedding present, and it occurred to her that he must be loaded if he could afford to be so generous towards his nephew.

Everyone gathered in the driveway to see the bridal pair on their way and soon they came out of the house and ran towards the car as the guests pelted them with confetti. Nicky hugged Veronica while Richard shook hands with Alex, and then they were moving to the car in a flurry of good wishes. Nicky started to get in, but then she hesitated and turned back, her eyes searching the crowd. Sara felt her heart contract as her sister moved suddenly towards her.

'Sara, I thought you might like this,' she said hesitantly and offered her the wedding posy of white rosebuds.

Her throat gone suddenly dry, Sara reached slowly out to take it. Nicky looked searchingly at her bent head for a moment, then bit her lip and went to turn away.

'Nicky.' Sara's voice made her turn back quickly and then she was held close in her sister's arms. 'Be happy,' Sara said chokingly. 'Oh, Nicky, please, *please*, be happy.'

And then Richard was pulling her towards the car as Nicky stared at Sara's face in astonishment.

They were away at last and Sara walked quickly back into the garden. She looked at the posy wryly, then dropped it on one of the tables. Bouquets were for brides, not career girls. Still shaken by the sudden emotion of the last few minutes, she needed some time to herself before she could feel confident enough to face anyone again. She groped for her glasses, then remembered that Alex had taken them away. Curse the man, what had he done that for? Just because she'd been wearing them, she imagined. The other guests had started to filter back so she walked further on down the path to the boathouse. It looked as good as new; the roof had been replaced and the rest repaired and given a coat of paint that made it blend in with the background trees.

Leaning against it, she gazed into the water and thought of Nicky and Richard. She didn't even know where they were going to live. Now that they were married she would have to see the solicitor and arrange for Nicky's inheritance to be passed over to her. It shouldn't take long, it was only a question of formalities, she thought broodingly.

'A penny for them!' Alex's voice broke into her thoughts and she turned her head to see him standing only a few feet away.

'You're behind the times,' she said lightly. 'Inflation has put the price up to at least five pence now.' Then she added, 'I believe you have my sunglasses.'

'Ah, yes.' He patted his pocket. 'But I think I'll keep them for a while in case you're tempted to hide behind them again.'

'I shall need them on the drive back,' Sara pointed out.

His eyes narrowed. 'You surely don't intend to drive back to London today? You'll be much too tired. You must stay here tonight and go back tomorrow.'

Sara lifted her chin. 'Must?'

'That's what I said,' he replied calmly.

'And just what right have you got to give me orders?'

'None—yet.' He reached up and took off her hat so that her hair fell down, tumbling like shiny, molten gold around her face. 'But I intend to take a very particular interest in your future welfare.' He dropped the hat on the ground and took a purposeful step towards her.

'Oh, no!' Sara breathed defensively.

'Oh, yes!' He said forcibly as he took her in his arms and silenced any further protests. There was nothing tender about his kiss, it was as forceful as his personality and it left Sara feeling bruised and shaken. His voice rather uneven, Alex said softly, 'I've been wanting to do that again ever since you left here.'

So he did it again, very thoroughly, and it was only the sound of approaching voices that made him let her go. For a moment Sara was too stunned to move; she could only lean against the boathouse and stare at him, heart pounding, her eyes dazed under heavy lids, lips still parted from the pressure of his. Then she realised they were being watched, so turned hastily and began to walk along beside the lake. Nonchalantly Alex bent to retrieve her hat and strolled alongside her, just as if being caught in a passionate embrace was the commonest thing in the world.

Sara found that she wasn't so blasée and hurriedly tried to think of something to say to cover her embarrassment. 'Somebody said you'd given Richard a car for a wedding present,' she managed.

'It wasn't a new one, only second-hand, but I thought they might need something to get around in.'

'Where are they going for their honeymoon?'

'Not far. Only to the Peak District for a few days. Richard's missed quite enough of his studies already.'

'The—the Peak District?' Sara looked at him questioningly, remembering all too vividly their own journey into the area when they had followed the false trail.

Alex grinned. 'Yes, I was able to personally recommend it.'

They were hidden from sight now by the rich greenness of a large rhododendron bush, so he hooked her hat on to a convenient branch and caught her round the waist, pulling her to him. 'And now can we forget about those two and concentrate on us for a change?'

'Us? There's nothing between us to talk about,' Sara said bravely, determined to go down fighting.

'Isn't there? I rather think there is.' And this time he was gentle, tracing with his lips the outline of her closed eyes, the contours of her cheeks, the shape of her trembling mouth. 'Oh, Sara, Sara,' he murmured. 'I haven't been able to get you out of my mind. During the day I wonder what you're doing, who you're with. And at night.... Perhaps I'd better not tell you what I think about at night.' His eyes glinted down at her mockingly, but then they became serious, an intense force darkening them as his hand came up to stroke her hair and push it away from her face so that he could bend to kiss her ear, catching the lobe between his teeth and biting gently. 'I want you, Sara. You don't know how much.' His lips left her ear and continued down her throat, burning into her skin.

Sara gave a little shuddering moan and then pushed herself away from him, afraid that matters might get out of hand. 'Alex, please! Somebody might come.'

He gave a somewhat rueful grin and straightened up, pushing his hair back from his forehead. 'Sorry. It's just that you're so damn desirable, I find it hard to keep my hands off you. You don't have to go back to London today, do you? Surely you can stay until tomorrow? We'll go out and have dinner, somewhere quiet where we can talk. '

Sara stared at him, heart racing, knowing the proposition he wanted to make to her, realising that the answer she gave now was crucial. 'All right,' she whispered, 'I'll stay.'

He picked up her hands and carried them silently to his lips, but his eyes spoke volumes, so that she could hardly even think coherently. An incredible excitement gripped her as her brown eyes met his dark ones. Never before had she been so physically aware of a man; his kisses had lit a fire deep within her and some instinct told her that this was only a small flame compared with the blaze of passion that Alex would rouse in her when he took her completely. And that he meant to take her there was no doubt. Perhaps he might even come tonight when the house was quiet and she was alone in her room. A mixture of fear and anticipation made her start to shake and showed in her eyes, wide in her suddenly pale face.

'Sara! Oh, God, you're so lovely. And it's such a hell of a long time till tonight.' His lips met hers in a kiss that was brutal in its hunger, his hands gripping her shoulders as he drew her against him. Sara's arms wound round his neck and she returned the kiss with an ardour that could only increase his passion. She pressed herself against him, but it wasn't close enough. She knew with overwhelming certainty that she wanted to be a part of him.

Rather abruptly he raised his head. Sara could feel his heart hammering in his chest and it was several minutes before he could say raggedly, 'I got more than I bargained for then, didn't I?' He stroked her hair again and gave a ghost of a laugh. 'I think we'd better go back to the reception before I forget myself completely. Kissing you is like kissing a keg of dynamite!'

He twined his fingers in hers, his eyes smiling at her with undisguised warmth. 'Thank heavens we've got those two married off at last. I was afraid you'd never stop fighting me.'

Sara smiled rather shyly back, hardly believing that this tall stranger beside her could have come to mean so much in such a short time. 'It was kind of you to arrange the reception. You must let me know how much it cost so that I can. . . .'

His fingers tightened on hers. 'Sara,' he said, warningly.

She laughed. 'All right, if you insist.'

'I do. And I'm going to insist on a lot of other things too,' he added firmly.

But that was dangerous ground again, and Sara hastily changed the subject. 'I'm sure they must both be very grateful. I expect if the baby's a boy they'll name it after you,' she added lightly.

Alex lifted a long finger to trace the curve of her lips and answered only abstractedly. 'Oh, no, they'll probably name it after Veronica because it was her idea to invent it in the first place so you'd. . . .' He stopped abruptly, suddenly aware of his own words and the incredulous look that was slowly dawning on Sara's face.

'What—what did you say?' Her hand broke free from his and she took a step away from him. The look of disbelief gradually changed to one of angry certainty. 'You made it up! There isn't any baby at all. Is there? Is there?' She almost shouted when he didn't answer immediately.

'Damn!' Alex raised his face to heaven as he cursed himself for a fool. Then, ruefully, 'No, there isn't. I intended to tell you, of course, but not until we'd sorted ourselves out.' He saw the look of fury in her eyes and added hastily, 'We had to do it, Sara. You were making the two of them completely miserable and for no good reason. Veronica happened to say that the only way to get your permission would be if Nicky was pregnant, and when you insisted on being stubborn I let you think it was so.'

'Let me think! You lied to me. You rotten....'

'No!' Alex cut in. 'I didn't lie to you. I simply told you they'd *got* to get married and your imagination filled in the rest.'

'Don't try to wriggle out of it that way. You know darn well what you implied. God, and to think I believed you! Let you see how much it mattered....' She turned away, filled with such a fierce rage that she wanted to strike out at him.

'Sara.' He came up behind her and put his hands on her shoulders, but she shook him off, twisting out from under his hands and turning to face him again. 'Keep away from me, you—you louse! Did Nicky know about this? Did she?'

'She does now, although she didn't know at the time that I intended to use it as a last resort.'

'That's right—if you can't win fairly by all means go ahead and lie and cheat!' she said scathingly.

A muscle in Alex's jaw tightened and she knew that she had flicked him, but he said brusquely, 'Be your age, Sara. What do you think would have happened if you hadn't let them marry? They would have been unhappy and miserable and you'd probably have provoked exactly the same situation anyway. But they don't matter now, they're on their own. What's important now is us.'

'If you think I ever want to even speak to you again after this, you're crazy! As far as I'm concerned you can go to hell and stay there. Where's my hat?'

She tried to reach past him, but he caught hold of her arms, holding her so that she couldn't get free, although she beat furiously against him with her fists.

'Sara, we've got something going for us and I'm damned if I'm going to let you break it up because of that foul temper of yours.' He tried to make her listen, but she wouldn't, covering her ears with her hands and refusing to look at him, until in the end he lost patience and pulled her roughly into his arms to get through to her that way.

At first she continued to struggle, then suddenly went limp in his grasp. When at last he raised his head her eyes looked into his in icy derision. 'You're just like all the others,' she said contemptuously. 'There isn't a man alive who doesn't believe he can use sex to get through to a woman, to bring her round. But not this time. Not any more. You made your faux pas just a little bit too soon for that to work!' And she turned on her heel and strode purposefully away.

# CHAPTER SEVEN

VERONICA was standing in the driveway saying goodbye to other guests, so Sara was able to take her leave quickly and get in the car. In order to get out into the road she had to first reverse, but when she went to move forward again she saw that Alex was standing in her path, effectively blocking the way.

Winding the window down, she said impatiently, 'Will you please get out of my way?'

'When I'm good and ready. If you drive off in that temper you'll have an accident before you've gone more than a mile.'

'I am *not* in a temper!' she snapped in a fury that belied her words, 'And even if I was, I'd still be capable of controlling this car.'

He came round to the side and leaned his head right through the window so that she hastily backed away. 'You forgot these.' He dropped her hat and her sunglasses on to her lap. 'And I believe this is yours too.'

Sara had thrown her hat on to the back seat, but now he held out Nicky's flowers. The scent of the roses drifted up to her nostrils and she bent her head to feel the softness of the petals against her skin. For a moment her eyes closed as she let the rich fragrance fill her.

'Sara, give me ten minutes to pack and then I'll follow you down the road. We'll stop somewhere along the way and have dinner—talk this out.' Alex's voice was as urgent as his eyes.

Slowly she raised her head to look at him, her loose hair and the softness of the roses giving her an ethereal loveliness, but then her face hardened and she thrust the flowers back at him. 'No. You went too far this time. Now get out of my way or I'll run you down.' Putting the car in gear she accelerated forward and Alex had to step hastily back to avoid having his feet run over.

For a mile or so Sara continued to drive fast, but then she slowed down as anger gave way to a feeling of unhappy frustration. To have been raised to such heights of dizzy expectancy and then to find that this man who had come to mean so much had cheated her! She drove a little further and then pulled on to the grass verge at the side of the road, her head throbbing so much that she raised her fingers to her temples to try to ease it. Only this afternoon had she fully realised just how much she was attracted to him. He had said that he'd thought about her while they'd been apart, and she had to admit that her thoughts had been equally full of him. There was a strength and certainty of purpose about him that she found completely overwhelming. At first she had tried to fight it, antagonised by his dominating personality, but today she had surrendered, and with the surrender had arisen a need that could only be satisfied by giving herself to him completely. She didn't know where the need came from, only that it was there, and that only this one man who had provoked it would be able to fulfil it.

She tried to tell herself that it was just physical, that by throwing herself into her work she would forget him, but reluctantly she had to admit that it wasn't so. She had tried to bury herself in her work during the last week and it hadn't been any use, so what was the point of fooling herself? After this afternoon she knew that she couldn't just drive away and never see him again. Her skin still burned from his touch, her mouth ached from the force of his kisses. She gripped the steering wheel until her knuckles showed white. This was crazy! She was a grown woman of twenty-six, wasn't she? Not some giggling teenager mooning over her first romance. But grown women of twenty-six could still fall for someone, couldn't they? And they were definitely old enough to take a lover.

Resting her throbbing head on the wheel, Sara tried to come to terms with her conscience. She knew lots of girls who lived with their boy-friends; it happened all the time, and often the relationships lasted for several years, until one of the partners got tired of the arrangement or found someone new. And then there were no messy divorces, no children to have their lives split in two. And let's face it, marriage among her contemporaries was definitely old hat; it was only the middle-aged and the very young, like Nicky and Richard, who still thought there was anything in it. Her mind rebelled against being tied down, and yet her body yearned for the closeness of Alex's. She wanted him as much as he wanted her, and the choice was hers; to drive on or to go back. To carry on alone as before or to yield to this overpowering need of him that was stronger than anything she had ever felt for a man.

When Alex drove along the road a quarter of an hour later, he saw Sara leaning calmly against the side of her car which was still parked on the verge. He pulled up in front of her and strolled back. Her hair was still loose about her shoulders, but she had replaced the sunglasses. 'What happened?' he asked her.

Sara shrugged. 'The engine just suddenly cut out.'

'Can't you fix it? Don't tell me you forgot to take car

mechanics when you graduated in Women's Lib.,' he said derisively.

'If I could fix it I wouldn't be here,' she rejoined tartly.

Taking his time, Alex slid behind the wheel and tried the engine. It was completely flat, lifeless. 'You'd better come with me and I'll give you a lift to the nearest garage.'

He got out and Sara retrieved her bag before locking the car and walking beside him without speaking to the Aston Martin. She stayed silent as he drove along the road, taking off the glasses to look studiously out of the window at the trees which were just starting to glow with the greenness of new leaves, at the little streams that tumbled whitely down the hillsides towards the distant blue of the lakes. They must have been driving for nearly ten minutes before Alex suddenly cursed under his breath and swung the car off the road and down a farm track before pulling up with a jerk.

'This is ridiculous!' He leaned over and drew her to him. 'Sara, I'm damned if I'm going to let your stubborn pride come between us any longer. You've driven me mad long enough!' And then she was in his arms, his muscles tightening to withstand the opposition that never came. Slowly he relaxed, looking at her questioningly and finding in her face a reassurance that took his breath away. He laughed softly, the light of triumph again in his eyes as he cupped her chin in his hand. 'You minx! I'm crazy about you, do you know that? You make me so furious with you that I want to take you across my knee and spank you like a child, but then you look at me half afraid, half trusting, and I want to hold you close and comfort you. But when I get you in my arms, comforting you is the last thing I want to do.'

'Oh? What do you want to do, then?' Sara asked innocently.

He grinned, sure of her now. 'Don't pretend you don't know or I might be tempted to show you.' Then more seriously, 'There's no going back now, my darling. You're mine, and I intend to claim you just as soon as I can. Oh, my dearest girl, I love you so much.'

His head came down to kiss her, but Sara pulled a little away from him, eyes wide in her startled face. 'What—what did you say?'

Alex smiled in amusement. 'Don't look so surprised. I've been in love with you ever since that day I let you believe that Nicky was pregnant. It was when I saw how much you cared about her that I realised just what all those crazy emotions I'd been experiencing really were. I'd known how much I wanted you all along, of course, but it wasn't until then that I knew I couldn't live without you.' His lips found hers and traced their outline in little kisses that left her breathless. 'For once, my love,' he said half-mockingly, 'you seem bereft of words.'

Tremblingly she raised her right hand to touch his face, letting her hand explore the planes of his cheeks, the firmness of his lips and strong chin. He turned his head slightly to kiss her palm, then looked at her questioningly. 'Sara?'

She knew what he wanted, of course; he wanted her to tell him in turn that she loved him, but his avowal had completely astounded her, thrown her thoughts into a turmoil. Did she love him, or were these feelings inside her purely physical, to be assuaged and then forgotten? She had thought herself in love before and it had come to nothing, and she was afraid now to commit herself, to make a statement that she wasn't sure was true. So instead she smiled rather mistily and said, 'Just think, if that lorry driver hadn't backed into my car so that we had to travel together this might never have happened.'

To her surprise Alex looked slightly shamefaced. 'Ah, yes, the lorry driver.' He took her hand and began to play with her fingers. 'I'm afraid I have a confession to make about that.'

'Confession?' she asked in puzzlement.

'Yes. You see, I bribed the driver to back into you. I had no intention of sitting in some hotel waiting until you saw fit to get in touch with me, so I decided to make sure you didn't leave me behind.' As he spoke he watched her warily, ready to catch her hand if she tried to let fly at him.

Indignation did kindle in Sara's eyes for a moment, but then she gave a gurgle of laughter. 'I suppose I ought to have guessed! It's just the kind of trick you'd pull to get your own way, but I didn't know you well enough at the time to realise it.' She bent down to pick up her bag and took something from it. 'As we seem to be at confession time, I suppose I'd better own up too.' Looking up at him mischievously, she opened her hand to display something wrapped in tissue paper.

Intrigued, Alex took it from her and opened the tissue to find a rather greasy metal nut.

'It's from the battery of my car,' Sara explained. 'I took it off so that I'd have an excuse to wait for you.'

'Supposing I'd decided to stay at Appleberry and not followed you?'

Rather unsteadily she answered, 'That was a chance I had to take.'

'But if I hadn't come along—would you have gone

back to Appleberry? Would you, Sara?' he asked insistently, his eyes searching her face.

She looked away. 'I—I don't know.' Then she smiled. 'But it doesn't matter, because you came.' Leaning across, she kissed him gently on the mouth. His lips fastened on hers compulsively and the kiss that had started out so tenderly ended with Sara clinging to him as the world slowly stopped spinning around her.

'Darling.' Alex's voice was uneven in her ear. 'I'm going to have that nut gold-plated and set with a diamond so that you can wear it as an engagement ring.'

Sara tensed beneath his hands. 'An engagement ring?'

He put a long finger under her chin and tilted her face so that he could see her. 'Of course. We're going to be married just as soon as it can be arranged.'

'*Married?* But I thought you only wanted to. . . .'

'To what?' His expression changed to one of astonishment. 'Good God, did you really believe that I only wanted to go to bed with you? What kind of man do you think I am? No wonder I've had such a hell of a time pinning you down! No, my lovely little idiot, my intentions are strictly honourable. We're going to be married, and not in some five-minute ceremony in a registrar's office,' he added firmly. 'We're going to have a white wedding with all our friends and relations there to wish us happiness. I want everyone to know how much you mean to me.' With a gentle hand he stroked the side of her face so that she quivered with awareness.

'And after the wedding?' she said unsteadily.

'We'll go on honeymoon—a month at least. Perhaps to the West Indies; you must choose. And when we get back we'll look round for a house. My flat's quite large, but we can live in yours till we find somewhere if you'd prefer it.'

'And my job?'

'You'll give that up, of course. I'm not exactly a millionaire, but I have enough for both of us.' He spoke emphatically, certain that she would be happy to fall in with his wishes, almost as if he was doing her a favour by taking away the one thing, other than Nicky, that had really mattered to her for so long.

Slowly she straightened and sat back in her seat, her face grave but determined. Trying to be reasonable, she said, 'Alex, my job means a lot to me, I've worked hard for years to get where I am and I don't want to give it up.'

'But, darling, I've already said it isn't necessary for you to go on working. I want you waiting for me when I get home at night,' he added firmly.

'Please try to understand, Alex. I *need* to work,' Sara said urgently. 'I'm used to the stimulus; meeting people, being creative.'

'And do you think you won't find that in marriage?' he interrupted brusquely. 'Of course you will. You'll find that there won't be enough hours in the day once we find a house and start a family. Sara, look at me,' he commanded when she quickly turned her head away. 'I want a full-time wife, Sara, not someone who's tired out in the evenings and can think of nothing but the problems she's got to face the next day. I've seen relationships like that and they seldom work out.' His voice hardened. 'I suppose what it comes down to is whether you care more for your job or for me.'

'Would you give your job up for me?' she asked defensively.

'Yes, if I had something else to take its place. But it's different for a man.'

'Is it?'

'Of course it is. He's the breadwinner,' he said tersely.

'Only because tradition dictates it. But I'm not asking *you* to give anything up, it's the other way round. And I'm afraid the price is too high.' She sat silently for a moment, but when she raised her face to his her eyes were determined. 'I'm sorry, Alex. I've been fighting for that job for six years, you I've only known for a few weeks. I'll live *with* you, but I won't live *through* you.'

'And just what is that supposed to mean?'

'It means that I'll move in with you, live with you, if you still want me, but I won't marry you on your terms. My work and independence mean too much to me for that.'

There was a short, shattering silence. 'What the hell kind of offer is that?' Alex asked fiercely.

'It's not one I'm in the habit of making,' Sara replied rather tartly.

'I want a wife not a mistress, Sara,' he said bluntly.

She winced at his choice of words, but stuck to her guns. 'I'm sorry,' shaking her head.

There was a bitter look of hurt rejection in Alex's eyes and his mouth twisted in cruel irony. 'It's almost funny, isn't it? The first time I've ever offered marriage to a woman and I get it thrown back in my face.' He sat back in his seat and reached for a cigarette, drawing on it viciously.

Unable to look at him, Sara could only stare unseeingly through the windscreen, her hands clasped tightly in her lap. She longed to comfort him, to take that look out of his eyes—and it would have been so easy to do, so easy to say she hadn't meant it, that she'd do what he wanted. Digging her nails into her palms, she forced herself to stay still, to let him be the first to speak.

'So you want us to live together,' he said at last. 'Want me to live in the knowledge that if anything happened to upset you there'd be nothing to hold you back from walking out on me. That I could come home at night and find you gone.'

'No, I wouldn't do that to you, Alex. I care about you too much to just walk out.'

He looked at her then, his eyes dark, unreadable. 'Care—but not love?'

Slowly she hung her head, unable to look him in the eyes.

'And what if I say it's marriage or nothing?'

'Say nothing, then,' she answered huskily.

He looked away from her, his face bleak. 'All right,' he said grimly after a moment, 'so we'll do it your way. But I'll move in with you; that way you won't be able to just pack up and leave. And there'll be no need to wait. I'll move in tomorrow.'

Tomorrow! Sara looked at the firm set of his jaw and decided to keep quiet, her mind a welter of mixed emotions: a sort of incredulous pleasure because she'd won, dismay at the speed with which he wanted to take up her offer, and a growing apprehension at what tomorrow would bring.

Alex drove her back to her car, replaced the nut on the battery and waited while she tried the engine. When it fired he said casually, 'I'll bring my gear round about eight tomorrow evening. See you then.' And he turned and strode calmly back to his car.

A distant church bell chimed eight times just as Sara zipped up her skirt. Frantically she pulled on a soft lamb's wool sweater before recombing her hair and making sure her make-up wasn't smudged. Then she went to throw the three different outfits she had rejected back into the wardrobe anyhow, but remembered in time that Alex would be sharing it and hastily picked them up to put them away properly. She still wasn't completely happy with what she was wearing— what did one wear on an occasion like this, for heaven's sake? But there wasn't time to change again anyway, he might be here at any minute.

As it was Sunday she had spent the whole day cleaning the place up and making space for Alex's things, and she had left dressing until after she'd put the dinner to cook in the oven. But there were still a thousand things she wanted to do, that kept occurring to her. He would probably have books and records, but her shelves were already bulging. Perhaps she ought to clear some of her things into Nicky's old room. She started to sort some books out when she noticed a cookery book and panicked because she hadn't turned down the oven. Frantically she ran into the kitchen and almost burnt her hand in her haste—but it was all right, she must have done it before she changed.

This was crazy! Sara forced herself to sit down in the kitchen to try to relax. Her heart was hammering in her chest and she felt almost sick with anticipation. All day she'd been rushing around, going out to find shops that were open on a Sunday to get food for dinner, taking her washing to the launderette to get it out of the way. The smell of the food caused her stomach to make protesting noises and she realised that she had been too tense and het up to eat all day, after an extremely restless night and the long drive back from the Lake District yesterday. Going back to the sitting-room, she replaced the books in their shelves; if Alex brought any with him they could arrange them together. Deliberately she tried not to think of what was going to happen, although her wayward mind seemed to return to it every five minutes. The reasons for and against she had gone over and over and felt completely justified in what she was doing. So why did she feel as if she was going to commit a crime? And why did she keep wanting to run out of the flat and hide herself away somewhere?

By the time the bell finally rang at a quarter to nine, Sara's nerves were a taut string of expectancy. Counting to ten first, she made herself go slowly to answer it. Alex was leaning negligently against the jamb, carrying a briefcase, an overcoat over his arm and a bulging holdall at his feet.

'Hallo. Sorry I'm late,' he said blandly. 'Had to go into the office to settle a few things that had cropped up while I was away.'

As he bent to pick up the holdall the door to the flat opposite opened and the rather nosy woman who lived there came out. Sara caught hold of Alex's sleeve and pulled him hastily inside, slamming the door behind him.

He looked startled. 'Do you always welcome your guests like that—or only your lovers?' he asked rather sardonically.

'It's that old cat across the hall,' Sara explained. 'If she'd seen you it would be all over the building in no time.'

'So what? She's bound to find out about our—er—arrangement sooner or later. You're not embarrassed about it, are you?' he added, giving her a searching look.

'No, of course not,' Sara replied with a brave show of confidence. 'I hope you haven't eaten because I've cooked dinner. Why don't you just leave your things there and we'll have it straightaway, shall we? That's unless you'd rather unpack first, of course,' she added hastily.

'No, suits me fine.' He dropped his coat and case on to a chair and followed her into the kitchen. 'Smells appetising. Are you a good cook?'

'I get plenty of practice with the plain stuff, casseroles and things, but I don't have much time to try anything exotic,' she told him as she took the food from the oven.

'No, I don't expect you do,' he said drily, and Sara turned quickly to look at him, expecting to find a sarcastic expression on his face, but he was looking round the room. She put the dish on the table and sat down opposite him. 'Do you always eat in the kitchen?'

'Either here or in front of the television; the flat doesn't run to a separate dining-room.'

He frowned. 'That's unfortunate. I have to entertain quite a few overseas customers.'

'You could always take them out for a meal,' Sara pointed out sharply.

'Yes, but they like to see the Englishman in his natural habitat, makes them think they're really getting to know the people.'

They began to eat and a silence fell between them that to Sara's tattered nerves seemed to go on and on. To break it she asked the only safe question she could think of. 'What were the problems you had to sort out at the office?'

Alex's eyebrows rose mockingly. 'What a very wifely question!' He explained more fully and this got them through to the dessert stage. 'Richard phoned me this afternoon, by the way,' he told her as he took a couple of forkfuls of the strawberry cheesecake she had so carefully made and then pushed it aside. 'He said they'd arrived safely and asked me to look out for a flat for them in London. I suppose the sort of flat they'll be able to afford will largely depend on whether you intend to hand over Nicky's money.'

'I haven't decided that yet. What's wrong with the cheesecake?'

'Hm? Oh, nothing, I suppose. I'm just not very keen on it.'

'I'll try to remember that in future,' Sara said rather caustically. 'Would you like a coffee?'

'No, thanks. I suppose being a liberated woman you expect me to help wash up?'

'I'll let you off tonight,' she replied, trying to keep her voice light. 'I expect you'd like to unpack. I've cleared out some drawers and part of the wardrobe for you. You don't seem to have brought very much?' she added on a questioning note.

'No, I only had the time to bring a few things to last me until I got round to sorting everything out. Where's the bedroom?'

'Through there, and the bathroom's next door.' Sara turned hastily away so that he couldn't see the flush that had come to her cheeks. He was so calm and emotionless, almost as if he handled this kind of situation all the time. And perhaps he did, she thought cynically as she began to wash the dishes. Which was just as well, because she hadn't the faintest idea how to go about things.

'Finished?' Alex came back conveniently just as she was hanging up the tea-towel. 'Let's go to bed, then, shall we? You can have the bathroom first, if you like?' He spoke quite matter-of-factly, his face expressionless, and didn't seem to hear Sara when she choked.

'But—but it's hardly ten o'clock,' she managed to stammer. 'Surely you don't want to go yet?'

'Well, it is what I came here for,' he pointed out reasonably. 'And besides I have a full day tomorrow.'

'Yes. Yes, of course.' Rather numbly Sara went into the bedroom to undress and put on a white towelling robe before going into the bathroom. When she came out he was in the bedroom and she quickly turned her back while he went to take his turn in the bathroom. She put on her most seductive white nightdress and negligee. There hadn't been time to buy a new one and she had changed her mind a dozen times, especially about the colour, before deciding which one to wear. Switching on the bedside lamps, she turned off the main light and then sat in front of the big round mirror on her dressing table while she brushed her hair with a trembling hand. Her reflection stared back at her, the brown eyes wide and dark in her pale face.

It was at that precise moment that she knew with utter certainty that she couldn't go through with it. If Alex had been loving and affectionate, if he'd taken her in his arms and kissed her as he had before.... But he was being so cold-blooded and—and businesslike about the whole thing. She couldn't do it, not like this.

Alex came out of the bathroom whistling and wearing a dressing-gown. Sara suddenly remembered that he never wore pyjamas. 'It's rather dark in here, isn't it?' He turned on the main light again and strolled over to the bed. 'What time do you like to get up?' he asked casually as he picked up an alarm clock he'd brought with him. 'I usually set mine for six-thirty.'

'That—that will do fine,' she said unsteadily.

'Good.' He began to undo the dressing-gown and Sara hastily glued her eyes to the floor. 'Aren't you ready?' he asked, and when she dared to raise her eyes she saw that he was sitting propped up against the pillows, his hands behind his head, watching her, the muscles in his shoulders standing out and making her realise just how much stronger than her he must be.

Tremblingly she got to her feet. 'Alex, I—I. . . .'

His eyes appraised her, slowly, appreciatively. 'Come here,' he ordered.

Slowly she walked to the other side of the bed. 'There's—there's something I have to tell you,' she began, determined to go on, but terrified of what he might do when she told him she'd changed her mind, especially when things had got this far.

Misunderstanding what she was going to say, he gave a twisted grin. 'Sara, this is no time for confessions from your murky past. I don't give a damn what you did before you met me. It's here and now that I'm concerned with.' He lunged forward and caught her wrist, pulling her down on to the bed and putting his weight across her. 'The time for talking's over, my sweet.'

His hand began to undo the negligee, she felt the smooth hardness of his chest against her skin and then she plunged wildly away from him. 'No! Alex, please!' But he still had hold of her wrist.

'What's the matter?' His eyes narrowed. 'Don't try and play games with me, Sara, or I'll teach you some you didn't even know existed.'

'No, it's just. . . .' Panic-stricken, she tried to think of something that would pacify him, make him let go of her. That it was no use appealing to him was more than obvious. 'It's just the lights. Please let me turn them off.'

Looking at her quizzically, he said, 'Not shy, are you?'

She hung her head, not letting him see her eyes. 'Yes, a little.'

He gave an amused laugh. 'I usually like to see what I'm getting. But okay, go ahead. Maybe you'll loosen up more in the dark.'

As soon as he let go her wrist, Sara walked as calmly as she could to the light switch by the door. The second she had switched it off she shot through the door and into the bathroom, slamming the door shut behind her, and turning the key in the lock. She leant against it, her heart beating wildly, her nerves at screaming point as she waited to find out what he would do. Supposing he burst open the door? Sara began to shake with fright at the thought.

His knuckles rapped peremptorily on the panel behind her head. 'I told you I don't like playing games, Sara. Now open the door and come on out.'

She turned and raised her voice to speak to him. 'It isn't a game, Alex. I'm sorry, but I changed my mind.'

'You did what? Have you gone off your head? You can't invite a man to live with you and get halfway into bed and then calmly tell him you've changed your mind!'

'Oh, Alex, please try to understand. I can't—not like this.'

'Are you coming out of there or do I have to break the door down and get you? Is that what your crazy mixed-up psyche wants? To be raped?' Even through the thickness of the door she could hear the savage menace in his voice.

'If you try it I'll lean out of the window and scream until the neighbours come.'

She heard him swear and then say grimly, 'What the hell are you trying to pull?'

'Nothing. I just realised that I'd made a mistake. I don't want to live with you after all,' she answered tremulously.

'You certainly picked a damnable time to find out! Look, Sara,' his voice became softer, 'why don't you come out and we'll talk it over. I won't even touch you unless you want me to.'

Like hell! she muttered to herself. 'No, I'm not coming out. Will you please just go away and leave me alone?'

His voice hardened again. 'You'll have to come out some time. Or do you intend to spend the whole night in there?' he asked sarcastically.

'If—if I have to.' She slid down to the floor, leaning the side of her head against the door. 'I'm sorry,' she said again. 'I know it's all my fault and you have every right to be angry, but please go away.'

There was a short silence and then she heard him move, go into the bedroom. A few minutes later he was back and again rapped on the door. 'Come on out.'

'No!' Her voice rose hysterically. 'I told you I'm not....'

'For heaven's sake, woman,' his voice interrupted her, 'look through the keyhole!'

Slowly she obeyed, taking out the key to see him standing a few feet away in the full glare of the sitting-room lights. He was fully dressed. Sara stared, uncertain what to do.

Alex must have guessed her thoughts because he said derisively, 'You're quite safe. You have nothing to fear from me after this.'

Reluctantly she stood up and unlocked the door. When she opened it he didn't move, just looked at her, his eyes and face contemptuous. 'What a coward you are, Sara! Afraid to commit yourself to marriage and even more afraid to share even a part of yourself. Well, I don't want anything from you that you can't give willingly and happily. You've told yourself so often that you don't need a man that you're too full of inhibitions even to go to bed with one. Why, Sara? Because you're too terrified of losing one iota of your precious freedom? Or is it because you know deep down that that's really what you want? To give yourself utterly to a man and let him have complete mastery of you. But I'm not going to hang around and let you make a fool out of me again. We've tried your terms and they didn't work. So now it has to be my way or nothing.'

Alex took his wallet from an inside pocket and extracted a card. 'This is the address of my flat.' He held it out to her, but she didn't move to take it. His mouth twisted and he dropped it on to a nearby table. 'When you decide what you want to do you can contact me and I'll let you know whether or not I'm still interested.'

He waited for her to speak, but when she didn't he gave her a scathing look that seemed to shrivel her inside, then he picked up his holdall and other belongings and let himself out of her flat, out of her life.

## CHAPTER EIGHT

It was hard to pretend that everything was as it had been before, but Sara tried hard over the next few weeks to convince herself that the even tenor of her life hadn't been broken beyond repair. She went to work and did her job as usual, and did it so efficiently that no one guessed her heart wasn't in it any more. The flat she put back to normal, replacing the clothes she had cleared out to make room for Alex's things, filling the gaps and wishing that she could fill the emptiness inside her as easily. The card he had left stayed on the table for some time until she resolutely picked it up and threw it in the waste paper basket.

But then she remembered that he had paid for Nicky's wedding reception. Being indebted to him was the last thing she wanted, so she fished the card out again and wrote him a stiff little note asking how much the reception had cost and also what she owed him for her share of the expenses on their never-to-be-forgotten journey to the Lake District.

A few days later she received a terse letter written in a thick, firm hand saying that the reception was part of his wedding present to Nicky and Richard, and that she owed him nothing for the journey. 'The lesson I learned was cheap at the price,' he finished caustically. If he hadn't added that last sentence Sara might have let it go, but it made her see red, so she wrote out a cheque that she thought would more than cover the amount adequately—and which took a large lump out of her savings—and sent it to him. The cheque came back by return post—torn into pieces. Going to her bank, Sara drew out four hundred pounds in ten-pound notes and sent them to him by registered post so that he would have no option but to accept the money. When she came home from work a couple of days later the registered envelope was lying on the doormat and had evidently been delivered by hand. Tremblingly she picked it up, the knowledge that he had been there matter.' And it had Alex's initials, so he must have got forty ten-pound notes—all torn in half!

There was also a typed note: 'Mr Brandon requests that you will cease bothering him further with this matter.' And it had Alex's initial, so he must have got his secretary to type it.

She left it then, afraid that if she took it any further he might come round and face her. The notes took ages to stick together and then she had to go round to the bank and explain that there'd been an accident and could they please take the notes back and pay them into her account.

May passed into June, but the warmer weather did little to cheer her; she found herself immune to the sun, the flowers in the parks and the excited discussions on holidays that went on around her in the office. Now that she no longer had Nicky to consider, she could have taken her holidays when she liked, but she felt no enthusiasm to make any arrangements even when she brought home lots of travel brochures from a travel agent's. The glossy hotels with their saunas and swimming pools only made her feel more than ever alone.

She made no move to have Nicky's legacy transferred to her; it was early days yet and if she found that the marriage was a good and lasting one she could always change her mind. But she heard nothing from her sister until almost six weeks after the wedding when Nicky phoned her at the flat one evening.

'We've got a bed-sitter now,' Nicky told her, her voice rather reserved. 'It's in Hampstead. We—we wondered if you'd like to come and have dinner with us one evening?' The invitation was hesitantly given, but Sara had no hesitation in accepting; more than anything else she wanted to be friends again with Nicky.

It was a beautiful evening when she drove out to Hampstead the following week, the deep gold of the setting sun reflecting dazzlingly on windows and shop fronts. It had been a hot day and she was wearing a thin, embroidered Greek-style shirt over a layered cotton skirt. In her lunch hour she had bought a bottle of wine and a potted plant, and these now reposed on the back seat as her contribution to the meal. She was unfamiliar with Hampstead and had to stop a couple of times to consult her A–Z guide, so was a little late in pulling up in front of the four-storeyed row of terraced houses where Nicky and Richard's bed-sitter was situated. The hall was rather dingy and smelt strongly of cooked cabbage. Peering at the fly-blown list of tenants, Sara found that the newlyweds were living on the top floor. Giving a slight groan, she began to climb the many flights of stairs, her footsteps noisy on the thin, holey carpet. Panting, she reached the top and rapped on the left-hand door behind which she could hear the sound of music and voices.

After a moment Richard opened the door and smiled rather shyly at her behind his spectacles. 'Hallo, Sara. I'm glad you could come.' He stood aside and ushered her in. 'Welcome to our humble abode.'

And it *was* humble, as Sara saw at a glance. The room was quite large, but it seemed to be cluttered with furniture; a double bed pushed into a corner, a massive old-fashioned wardrobe and dressing-table, and over by the dormer window a small table with four odd chairs round it. It was also set for four people, and it was only because of the few seconds' warning that this gave her that Sara was able to keep some sort of control over her features as Nicky came out of the tiny kitchen with Alex close behind her. He was wearing a tan suede jacket and trousers, and he looked very big and out of place. His expression didn't change when he saw her; he had evidently known she was coming.

'I didn't know this was going to be a party,' Sara remarked, keeping her voice light.

Alex's eyes challenged hers, daring her not to walk out or make a scene. Sara gazed back at him, not sure whether she could stand a whole evening in his dangerous company, the events of their last meeting too close and too strong.

Puzzled, Nicky looked from one to the other of them. 'Sara?' she said tentatively.

Sara blinked. 'Nicky, how are you? You're looking very well. These are for you,' she added, holding out the plant and wine.

Nicky gave a gurgle of laughter. 'We'll all get drunk tonight by the look of it. Alex brought a couple of bottles as well.'

Following her into the minute kitchen that was little more than a large cupboard, Sara watched as she placed the bottle of wine with the others in a gaily-coloured bucket of cold water. Marriage suited her, she realised, for Nicky looked very happy and somehow more mature, and she had lost quite a lot of her puppy fat already—probably by running up and down all those flights of stairs!

'Dinner won't be long. I've made spaghetti bolognese,

is that all right?' the younger girl asked rather anxiously.

'Mm, lovely.'

'I hope so, I've been practising for days,' Nicky confided.

Sara had to smile as she imagined poor Richard having to eat pasta every day until Nicky got it right. 'Can I help?' she offered.

'No, I think I've thought of everything, thanks. Oh, except could you give this tray of glasses to Richard? They aren't ours,' Nicky added. 'Alex let us borrow them when we left his flat.'

Sara's eyebrows rose. 'You were staying with him?'

'Yes, for a week or so until we found this place.'

Obediently Sara took the glasses in and Richard poured them each a sherry. It was terribly sweet, but Sara managed not to let her expression change as she drank it. Obviously Nicky and Richard, their palates not yet educated, found it exactly to their taste. She became aware that Alex was watching her, a look of amusement on his face as she struggled not to grimace at the cloying sweetness. They sat down at the table and Nicky piled their plates up with heaped strands of pasta and spoonsful of sauce.

Sara held up her hands in protest. 'Hey, that's enough! I shall never be able to get through all that lot!'

'Why? Are you on a diet or something?' Alex asked her tauntingly. 'Come to think of it, you do look rather thinner than when we last met. Quite peaky, in fact. Are you sure you're not working too hard?' he asked in mock solitude.

'I'm perfectly well, thank you,' Sara retorted tartly. He was sitting next to her on her left and she was acutely aware of the unavoidable pressure of his knee against hers under the small table. Hastily she asked Richard about their honeymoon, and with the help of the wine the atmosphere eased a little. Nicky was soon laughingly relating some amusing incident that had befallen them. Her face was flushed, but Sara noticed that Richard only let her have a couple of glasses of wine and then made her go on to lemonade.

'How are you managing?' Alex asked them.

'Quite well,' Richard answered in his usual calm voice. 'It's convenient for the college here, only takes about ten minutes in the car. And Nicky's got a job not far away,' he added with a grin.

Sara turned to her sister. 'Really? What kind of job?'

'Nothing very exciting. Just making the tea and running messages and that sort of thing for a drawing-office. But it's quite interesting and the people are very nice,' she added with a touch of defiance when she saw the fleeting look that came over Sara's face no matter how she tried to hide it.

'Sounds indispensable to me,' Alex broke in. 'There's a definite art to making tea. Did I tell you about one tea-lady we had at our office? We couldn't understand why we kept having so much absenteeism from stomach upsets until we found that the woman had been scouring the teapot and kettle out with some sort of acid. Seems she'd been doing the same thing at home for years and it hadn't had any effect on her at all. I reckon she must have had a cast-iron stomach.'

Richard helped Nicky to clear the plates after they'd finished the spaghetti, leaving Sara and Alex alone in a sudden silence.

'I didn't see your car outside,' she remarked stiffly,

picking up a fork and tracing patterns on the cloth with it.

'No, I came by cab. I'm going abroad shortly and the car's in for servicing.'

'Oh.' His knee touched against hers and she hastily moved her leg out of the way.

He looked at her sardonically and was about to say something but Nicky came back with the dessert and he stayed silent.

After the meal Sara insisted on helping with the washing-up and firmly closed the door to the kitchen behind them.

'I wanted to talk to you about your father's money, Nicky.'

'It's all right, Sara,' Nicky broke in before she could go on. 'I knew you wouldn't let me have it when you found out the truth. But it wasn't my idea, honestly it wasn't,' she added earnestly.

'No, I know. But you could have told me it wasn't true.'

'Yes, I suppose so. But I wasn't going to if it meant not getting married,' Nicky admitted honestly. 'And it doesn't really matter about the money because we're managing very well. Richard's father increased his allowance and sent us a fat cheque for a wedding present, so we're loaded.' She looked down and concentrated on washing the glasses. 'Although, ironically enough, I think the reason we pretended to use to get married might be true now.'

Sara stared at her in astonishment. 'What? You mean you think you're pregnant? But, Nicky, you've only been married a few weeks.'

'Well, I'm not absolutely certain yet, but I think I could be,' Nicky said blushingly. Then seeing Sara's shocked face, she said, 'It's what we want, Sara. We decided straightaway that we'd like to have a family while we're young. It's quite intentional, I assure you.'

Nicky sounded so serious and grown-up that Sara hardly recognised her, but there was an air of happy serenity about her sister that stilled many of her misgivings. Anyway there was nothing she could say, nothing she could do; Nicky belonged to someone else now and Sara had no hold over her any more. All she could manage was to extract a promise from Nicky that she would let her know when she herself knew positively one way or the other.

They sat around and chatted for a while longer, but at eleven Sara rose. 'I must be getting along. Thank you for dinner.'

Alex, too, got to his feet. 'And so must I. Perhaps you wouldn't mind giving me a lift, Sara?' he added, a glint in his dark eyes because he knew she couldn't very well refuse.

'Yes, of course,' she answered stiltedly, and they made all the conventional goodbyes.

The landing was very dimly lit and Alex stopped her as she was about to precede him down the stairs. 'You'd better let me go first. You'll fall and break your neck in those high heels.'

They got in the car and he seemed to fill it with his presence, his broad shoulders turned slightly sideways so that he could watch her. Rather tremblingly she inserted the key in the ignition.

'Would you like a cigarette?' he asked as she pulled away.

'No, thanks. I never smoke while I'm driving.'

'Very wise.' He lit one for himself and opened the window a little to let the smoke escape.

Sara forced herself to keep calm and asked as steadily as she could, 'Are you going abroad for long?'

'Two or three weeks. I have to go to France to follow up a possible contract and then on to West Germany.'

A silence fell between them after that until he told her which direction to take to reach his flat. It was in an imposing-looking court in a quiet avenue off Baker Street.

'Will you come up for a nightcap?' he asked as she drew up outside.

'No, thanks. I'm rather tired.'

'Still as big a coward as ever, Sara?' he asked softly.

Slowly she turned her head to look at him. The light from the street lamp shone through the window, accentuating the angles of his face, deepening his jaw-line and hardening his mouth, giving him a cruel, satanic look. 'Yes, I suppose so, if that's what you want to think,' she answered after a moment. 'I haven't changed, if that's what you mean. I still want the same things out of life. They just don't happen to be the same things that you want, that's all.'

'There's one thing that we both want,' he said with a harsh note creeping into his voice. 'Only you're too damned scared to let go of your inhibitions and find it out for yourself.'

'Please! Can't we just leave it?' Sara's hands gripped hard on the steering wheel. 'What's the point of going on? We both know it's a waste of time.'

'Is it? You can't deny your feelings for me so easily, Sara. You may not be sure in that crazy, mixed-up head of yours just what they are, but you know darn well that they're there. I only have to touch you and you go to pieces.'

'That isn't true.'

'Isn't it?' He reached out and drew her towards him, taking his time about it, letting her see the purposeful look in his eyes. His hand was burning hot as it travelled slowly up the material of her shirt, undoing the strings at the neck and sliding inside to caress her throat. 'Isn't it, Sara?' he asked again softly, his mouth only an inch or two away from her own.

She forced herself not to respond, to hold herself rigidly in his arms as his lips met hers, gently, caressingly. His kisses became deeper and then almost cruel as she stayed frozen beneath the hot demands of his mouth. His hand strayed down to fondle her breast and she began to tremble violently. As he felt it, his lips became more passionate, more importuning, but she still refused to yield to him, her body stiff and unbending, her lips stubbornly cold beneath his.

Alex let her go suddenly, his eyes boring into hers. Then without a word he swung himself out of the car and slammed the door behind him before striding purposefully into the entrance of the apartment building.

So it was over, finished. And now perhaps she could get back to being in control of her own life-style again, put Alex's disturbing memory out of her mind completely and just write him off as one of those experiences one has to go through in life. But it was a few days before she could bring herself to look at the whole episode objectively. Knowing him had taught her a lot; that she wasn't willing to sacrifice her career and her independence for marriage and security, and also that she couldn't blithely enter into a cold-blooded sexual relationship. So just what did she want? she wondered wryly. A man who would be warm and loving, but otherwise not make any demands on her time and her freedom, someone who stayed conveniently in the background? She smiled cynically to herself; that sounded more like a wife than a husband! And did she really want such a luke-warm affair when Alex had opened the door to show her what passion could hold? Gripping her bottom lip between her teeth, Sara tried to dull the aching desire that pulsed through her body. She had hoped that by exerting all her self-control when he had kissed her after dinner at Nicky's, she would have exorcised him for ever, proved to him that he no longer meant anything to her, and to herself that she didn't need marriage or any kind of sexual relationship to lead a happy and contented life.

But it wasn't going to be an easy job to forget him; she had tried in the last few weeks and had thought herself to be succeeding, then she had walked into Nicky's flat and it had all been for nothing. And he had known it, too, had been certain that a few kisses would make her give in completely, admit that he had mastered her. And it had taken an iron will-power to defy him, an effort that left her feeling drained and weak for days afterwards.

Sara phoned Nicky a couple of weeks later to offer a return invitation to dinner, and one look at her sister's radiant face was enough to tell her that her news had been confirmed and she was going to be an aunt. Without Alex the atmosphere was far more relaxed, and over a meal that Sara had tactfully made sure wasn't too elaborate, Richard became more loquacious than she had ever known him.

'After I've passed all my exams I'd quite like to take Nicky out to Africa to meet my parents, and I might even try to get a partnership out there,' he confided. 'It's a wonderful country, just great for kids.'

'You must come out there and visit us if we do settle there, Sara,' Nicky put in. 'That's if you can spare the time from your work, of course,' she added without sarcasm.

'Oh, I think I could manage it. It's not all work and no play, you know,' Sara returned lightly.

And as if to prove to herself the truth of this statement, she took up the open invitations that two or three men had given her and made dates to go to the theatre, concerts, night-clubs. It was fun and she enjoyed the new places and new company, or so she told herself very firmly. But when they kissed her goodnight or tried to take things further, she found that she just wasn't interested, there was nothing there. No touch to send her pulses racing, no spark to set her senses on fire and make her heart lurch within her.

Telling herself that the others just happened to be incompatible, she accepted the invitation of a rich and handsome Canadian whom she met through the advertising agency, and for a while it seemed that he might make her forget. But one evening over dinner at a fashionable restaurant it suddenly hit her that nothing was going to help—he was the wrong man, just as every man she would meet for the rest of her life would be the wrong man! With shaking hands she set down the glass she was holding. 'I'm sorry, I don't feel very well. Will you take me home, please?'

He was all concern and wanted to call a doctor as soon as they got to her flat, but she persuaded him that she'd be all right if left alone and presently he went away.

Slowly Sara took off her dress and shoes and then lay on the bed for a long while just gazing at the ceiling. When the doorbell rang she thought it must be the

Canadian returning to see if she was all right, so she pulled on a robe and went to answer it. The bell rang again, imperatively. Almost automatically she glanced at her watch; eleven o'clock. Surely he wouldn't come back at this hour? Putting on the chain, she gingerly opened the door a few inches. Her eyes flew wide in surprise; Alex was standing in the corridor, a grim, set look to his face.

'Let me in, Sara. I have to talk to you.'

'I—I thought you were abroad,' she stammered, her fingers still gripping the door.

'I came back last weekend,' he answered impatiently. 'Let me in, will you?' His eyes narrowed as he saw that she was partly undressed. 'Unless you've got someone in there, of course.'

Sara's face flushed and she quickly undid the chain and opened the door wide. 'There's no one here. Search the place if you don't believe me.'

'Just thought you might be conducting another experiment in your search for conjugal bliss,' he replied sardonically as he came in and shut the door behind him.

Her face paled, leaving two bright spots of colour high on her cheeks. 'Why don't you just say what you came to say and then get out?' she snapped angrily.

Alex ran a hand through his hair and said ruefully, 'I'm sorry, I hadn't meant it to start like this. I just can't seem to stop the sparks flying when I'm with you, can I?' Without waiting for her to answer, he went on, 'I'm afraid I have some bad news. It's Nicky. She fell down the stairs at their place and has been taken to hospital. Richard phoned me and asked me to let you know.'

Aghast, Sara could only stare at him for a moment, then, 'How badly is she hurt?'

'Pretty bad, I'm afraid. Richard said she was unconscious when he got to her and still hadn't recovered when they reached the hospital.'

'I must get dressed, go to her.' Running into her bedroom, Sara blindly pulled on a skirt and jacket, pushing her feet into sandals before hurrying to rejoin him.

They didn't speak again until they were in Alex's car and he was cutting his way surely through the late night traffic, driving as fast as he safely could.

'How long ago did it happen?' she asked anxiously.

'Almost an hour, I should think. She'll probably have come round by the time we get there,' he added consolingly.

But when they hurried into the hospital casualty department with its drab, cream-painted walls and rows of uncomfortable seats, they found Richard still sitting dejectedly alone, his face tense and worried. He stood up when he saw them and said at once, 'They won't tell me anything. She's been in there for ages and I've asked everyone who's come out, but no one will tell me what's happening.'

He was terribly upset, almost incoherent, so that Alex immediately went away to try and find someone in authority, while Sara took Richard's hand and persuaded him to sit down beside her.

'How did it happen?' she asked him, knowing that he could think of nothing else and hoping that talking about it might help.

'She was going down to put out the milk bottles and empty some rubbish. I would have done it myself, but I was studying and she didn't want to disturb me. Then she must have caught her heel in that worn stair carpet,

because I found her shoe still there when I heard the
crash and ran out to find out what had happened. She
was so still, Sara. For a moment I thought she was.…
I thought she was.…' His hand gripped hers convul-
sively. 'But then a girl came out of another bed-sitter
and said she'd been a nurse. She felt Nicky's pulse and
told me to get an ambulance. But she didn't open her
eyes or move, not once, all the way here.'

Sara comforted him as best she could, but turned
anxious eyes up to Alex when he came back some time
later.

'I managed to catch the Sister on duty,' he told them.
'Nicky's been taken down for X-rays and now they're
waiting for the results. They won't know anything for
a while, but she's promised to come and tell us as soon
as they do. So I suggest we go to the snack bar and have
something strong and hot. You look as if you need it,
old chap,' he said to Richard.

'But I can't. They might come while we're not here,'
Richard answered fretfully.

'I'll stay. I'll come and find you straightaway if there's
any news,' Sara told him, giving him a little push in
Alex's direction.

Taking him firmly by the elbow, Alex led him away,
talking to him, reassuring him.

Sara sat down again, by no means reassured herself,
looking up expectantly whenever a nurse or white-
coated doctor appeared through the anonymous swing
doors, but none approached her, always going about
their business or coming up to some other anxiously
waiting relative. When the two men returned she could
only shake her head. After a while, at Alex's suggestion,
she went to get herself a cup of coffee, trying to drink
it slowly to help the time to pass, but all the while want-

ing to get back in case there was any news. Putting down her empty cup, she rose to leave when Alex came into the room. The look on his face kept her frozen where she stood.

'They've asked Richard's permission to operate,' he told her bluntly. 'Evidently she's broken some ribs and they think a bone may have pierced her lung. They also suspect some internal injuries.'

The room, with its spartan tubular steel chairs and plastic-topped tables, started to spin. She swayed and Alex quickly caught her arm. 'Come on, Sara, bear up. You're tough enough to face this.'

'Am I?' she leant against him for a moment, then straightened and squared her shoulders. 'Yes, I suppose I am.' But there was a pallid look to her mouth as they walked back to rejoin Richard.

The next two hours were unadulterated hell. Occasionally patients were brought in, but with the early hours of the morning the place quietened and left them sitting together in a little pool of helpless anxiety. It was almost three hours before the tired-looking surgeon came through the doors and walked towards them.

'Mr French?' Richard had already risen to meet him, his face sharp with hope, with dread. 'Your wife is going to be all right, Mr French,' the surgeon went on. 'Luckily the broken rib hadn't perforated the lung but was pressing against it, and we've been able to put that right.'

A stab of intense relief filled Sara and she sagged back into her chair, but then she saw that the grave look hadn't left the doctor's face. Richard noticed it too.

'And the other injuries?' he asked sharply.

'Your wife is young and healthy, so we must hope for

the best, but you must be prepared for her to lose the child she is expecting.'

Richard blinked behind his spectacles and sat down abruptly.

'Is this a planned pregnancy?' the doctor asked him.

When Richard couldn't answer, Sara said it for him. 'Yes, it is. They want the baby very much.'

The doctor nodded approvingly. 'We'll do everything we can. If she manages to hold on for the next hour or so she should be all right.' Then he went away.

Alex put a hand on Richard's shoulder. 'At least Nicky's going to be okay, old son. You've got that to hold on to.'

'Yes. Yes, I know.'

Richard groped in his pockets for a handkerchief and Alex said firmly to Sara, 'We're not allowed to smoke in here, but I could do with a cigarette and I expect you could too. Let's go outside and have one, shall we?'

He took her arm and hurried her outside, not stopping until they had left the hospital and walked round to a tree-lined garden where the patients could sit out during the day. It had rained earlier in the evening leaving the clean sweet smell of fresh grass and wet earth still hanging in the air. The moonlight filtered through the leaves of the trees illuminating a gravel path along which they walked slowly.

'Will Richard be all right alone?' Sara asked after he had lit a cigarette for himself, she having refused one.

'Yes, best to leave him by himself for a bit. He's pretty shaken up by all this. Lord, what a mess! Richard should have insisted on taking the rubbish himself.'

'You can't blame Richard for it,' she said tightly. 'If anyone's to blame, I am. It's completely my fault.'

Alex swung round to look at her. 'You?' he exclaimed.

'Yes. If I hadn't been so insistent on them learning to be self-sufficient, if I'd let them have the legacy, they would have been able to afford somewhere decent to live, instead of on the top floor of that old house. There wouldn't have been any worn stair carpet to trip over, or any need to throw out rubbish. If I hadn't been so stubborn and selfish....'

'Sara, stop it!' Alex threw away his cigarette and took hold of her shoulders, shaking her gently. 'It's nonsense to blame yourself. It could have happened anywhere.'

She raised her head to look at him, her eyes tormented. 'Oh, Alex, she wants that baby so much. If she loses it....'

'I know.' He drew her head against his shoulder, holding it there, feeling her trembling against him. 'But they're young, Sara. It will be a terrible blow, but they'll bounce back, you'll see. They'll probably end up with a football team before they're finished.' His arm tightened around her. 'And I'm not going to let you cut yourself up inside by thinking it was all your fault. You did what you believed was best.'

Huskily Sara answered, 'The funny thing is that as soon as Nicky told me she really was pregnant, I told the solicitors to make the money over to her. She would have been getting it any day now. Ironic, isn't it?' she added bitterly.

Alex turned her round to face him again, but didn't let her go. 'Sara, torturing yourself isn't going to help anyone, least of all Nicky. All right, maybe you did make a mistake, but it happens to everyone at times. You do something from the best of motives and then it blows up in your face and there's no going back.' There was harshness in his voice as he spoke and his hands bit into her shoulders.

Sara looked up at him wonderingly. 'You sound as if it happened to you?'

'It did,' he agreed rather unsteadily. 'When I fell head over heels in love with the only woman I've ever wanted to marry and thought I could change you, mould you into the sort of woman I wanted you to be, instead of realising that I'd fallen in love with you for the very qualities I was trying to make you give up.'

Sara became very still beneath his hands, slowly raising her head to see his face. There was an intent look in his hard grey eyes. 'Alex....' she began.

'No, don't say anything. Not yet. I know we've started off all wrong, but at least give me a chance to put it right.' He paused for a moment, then said slowly, 'When you refused to marry me it made me so mad that I made up my mind to bring you to heel. That's why I was such a pig that night I was supposed to move in with you. I wanted you as my wife, not as a mistress, and I was determined to force you into doing it my way. I deliberately played the whole thing down, made out it was commonplace, left out all the love and warmth I so much wanted to show you, because I was sure that without it you wouldn't be able to go through with it. And I was right, you bolted like a rabbit to its hole.'

'What would you have done if I hadn't locked myself in the bathroom?' Sara asked curiously.

His mouth twisted in a wry grin. 'That was something I didn't dare think about. It was hard enough keeping up a pretence as it was. And even then the whole thing backfired on me. I'd made you admit you cared for me and I thought that after a couple of days you'd see reason and agree to marry me. But the days turned into weeks and it was then I realised what a hell I'd made for myself, so I badgered Richard into inviting us both to dinner. But I even made a mess of that, didn't I,' he added with bitter self-contempt. 'Instead of talking to you, telling you how much I needed you, I tried to show you. And you thought I was just trying to dominate you through sex again, and let me know in no uncertain terms just how far that was going to get me. Then I had to go abroad, and although I cursed it at the time, perhaps it was a good thing, because it gave me time to think and I realised a whole lot of things that I'd been too damn stubborn and obstinate to see before.'

'What things?' Sara asked, her voice dry in her throat.

'The first was that without you there would be no future in life, and the second, that although you can compromise in marriage you can't compromise with love.' He paused. 'But before we can start over again I have to know whether you still care enough.' His voice became urgent. 'You've always been honest with me, Sara, so tell me the truth. Could you love me?'

The moon went behind a cloud and he couldn't see her face as she gently disengaged herself from his hands and stepped a few feet away from him. For a long time she didn't speak, but when she at last turned towards him her face was troubled and her voice husky with emotion. 'Whether I love you or not doesn't matter, because even if I married you on your terms I don't think I'd be capable of giving you what you want. 'I'm—I'm not very good at close relationships, you see.' Painfully she tried to explain. 'I adored my mother, but she lost interest in me when she remarried and had Nicky, and then. . . .' She held up a hand as Alex made a movement to stop her. 'No, please, let me finish. When I was engaged my fiancé became so jealous when I was more successful than he was that he made me change my job. And then there was Nicky.' She shrugged helplessly. 'Well, you've seen what a complete failure I've been with Nicky.'

Alex came two swift strides towards her and took both her hands in his. 'You're no failure, Sara. You've got courage and loyalty, you're independent and not afraid to stand up for what you believe in. Okay, so maybe your mother didn't give you as much attention as you needed, but that was hardly your fault, and you should have been pleased when you found out what your fiancé was like before you married him. And as for Nicky, she's a very nice girl; just not the type you wanted her to be, that's all. But one I'll be very happy to have for my sister-in-law,' he added softly.

Sara's hand jumped in his and she tried to pull free, but he wouldn't let her go. 'It's not just that,' she told him unhappily.

Slowly Alex said, 'You told me once that you had had several offers of marriage but couldn't accept them. Why was that, Sara?'

For a moment she looked puzzled, but then her brow cleared. 'Oh, that was because I was paying off the mortgage on the flat and also struggling to pay Nicky's school fees. When they found that out they didn't want to know—naturally.' She shrugged. 'No, it's not that. It's. . . .' She hesitated, then said with a rush, 'You said you wanted a family, but I'm not sure that I'd be any good at that sort of thing. I'm not like Nicky, I don't have this urge to reproduce. I wish I did, but I'm afraid I'd be hopeless as a parent.'

She looked up at him anxiously and to her surprise
he laughed. 'Good lord, is that all? I was afraid you
were going to tell me something dire.' He gathered her
to him and said gently, 'No one knows what sort of
parent they're going to make until it actually happens.
It's something you have to learn as you go along, just
like every other part of living. And now,' he said firmly,
holding her a little away from him, 'would you please
answer the question? And don't tell me you've forgotten what it was, because I know darn well you haven't.'

Sara gave a ghost of a smile. 'No, I haven't forgotten.
How could I when you're holding me?' His face was
shadowed by the moonlight, but he could see hers
clearly as she lifted her face to him. 'Yes, Alex,' she said
steadily, 'I love you. I love you so much that I feel
empty and incomplete without you.'

His hands dug sharply into her arms so that she
winced and for a long moment he could only stare unbelievingly into her face. When he did speak he took
her completely by surprise. 'Do you know anything
about computers?' he asked rather raggedly.

'Computers?' Startled, she tried to grope for a reply.
'As much as any layman, I suppose. We did some advertising for a computer firm once, but why on earth. . .?'

'Because I need a part-time Public Relations officer,'
he told her. 'Someone willing to travel anywhere to
liaise with customers, someone who can sell my company to the biggest organisations in the world. Well?'
he added impatiently. 'Don't just stand there goggling
at me, woman. Do you think you could handle it?'

Sara swallowed. 'Yes. Yes, I know I could.'

'And will you accept the position?'

She raised her eyebrows. 'What is the salary?'

A devilish look came into Alex's eyes. 'Very good, and

there are some extremely interesting side benefits.'

'Oh? Do I get a car?' she asked suspiciously.

'Of course. An Aston Martin.'

'Hm, that certainly sounds tempting. How about holidays?'

'Very generous. In fact the job actually starts with a working holiday in which you'd be given night and day instruction in your new duties,' he added wickedly. 'Well, will you take it?'

'I don't know. It all sounds just too good to be true,' she said with mock hesitation.

'Ah,' he said with a reluctant sigh. 'I see you've guessed it. There is one small drawback—you have to sleep with the boss!'

'In that case I'll definitely take it,' Sara said firmly, and put her arms round his neck as he pulled her to him and kissed her as a woman should be kissed, moulding her body to his own and letting her know how much he needed her. In the warmth and safety of his arms, Sara felt any doubts she might have dissolve away. The years ahead might be stormy on occasion, they were both too strong-willed for them not to be, but at least they'd be together, working for a common aim. It might not be happy for ever after, but Sara knew with utmost certainty that the heights of passion would be glorious and worth all the rest. Something of her thoughts must have communicated to him, for Alex kissed her as if he would never let her go, making the world whirl giddily round her until there was nothing left but the demanding sensuousness of his mouth, the need to hold herself ever closer to his lean hardness.

The sound of their names being called penetrated to Sara's ears at last and she rather dizzily tried to free herself.

Alex immediately pulled her back and started to kiss her neck, her eyes. 'No, stay here,' he ordered thickly, his breathing ragged.

'But someone's calling us. It must be Richard.'

He straightened at once, pushing his hair back from his forehead, then taking her hand to lead her towards the front of the hospital where Richard was looking for them.

He caught sight of them and came running across the tarmac excitedly. 'It's all right. The doctor says Nicky's past the danger point. She isn't going to lose the baby!'

And somehow they were all standing there, laughing and crying, hugging one another with happiness in the middle of the hospital courtyard at four o'clock in the morning.

'They let me see her for a minute when she came round, but she's asleep now. But we can all come back tomorrow.' Richard was almost babbling in his delight and relief.

'In that case I think we'd better take you home so that you can get some sleep.' Alex remarked as he shepherded them towards the car.

They dropped Richard off and then drove through the quiet streets just as the first pink streaks of dawn began to appear in the sky.

'Your place or mine?' Alex asked, an amused glint in his eyes.

Sara laughed. 'Oh, no. If we're going to get married, then we'll do the thing properly. Besides, it'll pay you back for what you did to me.'

'Hoist with my own petard,' Alex said with a rueful grin.

'We ought to send Nicky some flowers,' Sara suggested.

'Mm. I'll phone up the office and leave a message on the recorder for my secretary to do it as soon as she comes in. Then Nicky should find the flowers when she wakes up.'

'That would be lovely,' Sara agreed. After a moment she added casually, 'Your secretary—what's she like?'

'Oh, she's twenty-two, with red hair and a fantastic figure, and boy, is she fast! Her typing and shorthand speeds are phenomenal.' Alex added, after a significant pause, as they pulled up outside her flat.

'Oh!' Sara said rather hollowly. 'She sounds too good to be true.'

'She is,' Alex replied mockingly. 'She's really forty-five and married. But it was worth making her up to hear that note of jealousy in your voice.'

'Jealousy!' Sara exclaimed indignantly. 'Of course I'm not!' Alex leant over her to undo her safety strap and his lips just happened to touch the curve of her chin and went on to explore the hollows of her cheeks, the lobe of her ear. She gave a little moaning sound and said weakly, 'Well, perhaps just the tiniest bit jealous.'

He laughed softly, his mouth against her neck, and said happily, 'You know, Sara, I'm going to make a female chauvinist of you yet!'

# The Warrender Saga

## The most frequently requested series of Harlequin Romances . . . Mary Burchell's Warrender Saga

A Song Begins    The Curtain Rises
The Broken Wing    Song Cycle
Child of Music    Music of the Heart
Unbidden Melody
Remembered Serenade
When Love Is Blind

Each complete novel is set in the exciting world of music and opera, spanning the years from the meeting of Oscar and Anthea in *A Song Begins* to his knighthood in *Remembered Serenade*. These nine captivating love stories introduce you to a cast of characters as vivid, interesting and delightful as the glittering, exotic locations. From the tranquil English countryside to the capitals of Europe— London, Paris, Amsterdam—the Warrender Saga will sweep you along in an unforgettable journey of drama, excitement and romance.

# The Warrender Saga

## The most frequently requested Harlequin Romance series

# Complete and mail this coupon today!

# What readers say about Harlequin Romances

"Your books are the best I have ever found."
P.B.*. Bellevue. Washington

"I enjoy them more and more
with each passing year."
J.L.. Spurlockville. West Virginia

"No matter how full and happy life might be,
it is an enchantment to sit
and read your novels."
D.K.. Willowdale. Ontario

"I firmly believe that Harlequin Romances
are perfect for anyone who wants to read
a good romance."
C.R.. Akron. Ohio

*Names available on request